TALES OF NEZURA
BOOK 1: THE ZEVOLRA

RANDALL FLOYD COOPER

Copyright © 2021 Randall F. Cooper All rights reserved

The characters and events portrayed in this book are fictitious. Any similarity to real persons, living or dead, is coincidental and not intended by the author.

No part of this book may be reproduced, stored in a retrieval system, or transmitted in any form or by any means, electronic, mechanical, photocopying, recording, or otherwise, without the publisher's written permission.

ISBN: 978-1-7369715-0-5
Printed in US
Cover Design: Anthony Valdez

Thank you to my family & friends who've supported me in so many ways. Thank you for reading, listening, and watching all of the works I've been a part of. Special thank you to my dad, my aunt, my grandpa, Kenzie, Angie, Natalie, Dylan, Nate, David, Tim, Kat, Dustin, and Palace. They've gone above and beyond in supporting my dream, and I don't know if I'd be doing what I'm doing if it wasn't for their encouragement and belief in me.

I dedicate this novel to my mom. I don't know if she would've liked this book, but I think she would. One thing I know for sure, she'd be thrilled that I published something.

NECROMANCER /ˈnekrəˌmansər/ - a person (wizard/witch) who practices magic with a focus on summoning skeletons.

PROLOGUE

The thirty-year-old King Mozer sat at the head of the long table in the Great Hall with his chin resting on his fist. Silver Navy admirals filled the seats inside the beige flagstone chamber, which had purple pennants hanging between tall, arched windows. The royal servants finished serving turkey, potatoes, and mead. Sitting on King Mozer's right was Lara, his tall, beautiful assistant who had been with his family before he was born. She was athletic and mighty at forty-five.

The feast ended as soon as it started. All twenty Silver Navy admirals inhaled their food.

"We enjoyed our meal this evening, yes?" Mozer's crooked lips pulled up into a grin.

Everyone at the table nodded and smiled.

"Good, now we don't have to waste any more time. There's important business to discuss."

The admirals straightened their posture and focused their attention on Mozer.

"Now, for the next few years, there's a project we have to start in order to defend ourselves against the necromancers. They're going to attack us again—there's no doubt about it—and they're going to be on the lookout for heavy artillery. Something so powerful, we wouldn't have a chance at defending against it. I want you to search every inch of the seas, lakes, and oceans in your outposts. We're going to be searching for skeletal remains, not just regular old bones, but the bones of something that died long ago, which existed before our time. A gigantic monster."

A snicker slipped out from one of the admirals.

Mozer halted his speech and pointed to the admiral, who stifled his laughter. "You. What's your name?"

"I'm Admiral Flannery, Your Highness."

"This is no laughing matter. Have you seen what a necromancer is capable of summoning?" Mozer asked.

"I thought they were just dirty people who summoned up the dead remains of animals?"

"Do you forget what happened when Akara stormed this castle?" Mozer screeched as Admiral Flannery trembled. "She took the dead from cemeteries and turned them into skeletal warrior armies. Imagine that all over again, but combined with a prehistoric monster!"

Lara gave Mozer a side glance, but Mozer cleared his throat and continued, "I was in a good mood, and then Admiral Flannery here tried to ruin that. So now, I have a request for him. Get up, right now."

Flannery scooted his chair back and stood up, facing the king with a slight frown.

"Please, step towards me." Mozer beckoned, but Flannery hesitated. "I don't have all vlarking night! Get in front of me now!" Mozer pointed in front of his feet.

Flannery hurried up to the king and bowed. "Your Highness, I'm sorry."

"I want everyone to look right now. Yes, all eyes on Flannery." He scowled. "What could I do to embarrass you in front of your peers?" Mozer asked, but there was no reply. "*I said,* what could I do to embarrass you in front of your peers!"

"I don't know, sire!"

"You've already embarrassed me by just existing! Now, what can I do to make your skin crawl?" Mozer raised his voice and moved forward, inches from Flannery's face. "Perhaps a tickle of the nose?" Mozer raised his finger and traced the bridge of Flannery's nose, causing Flannery to wince and back away. "I didn't say you could move! Come closer!"

Flannery leaned forward.

"Perhaps the tickle wasn't good enough." Mozer caressed the admiral's face. "Maybe a slap would suffice?"

Mozer smacked Flannery's cheek with so much force it knocked him over, and he collapsed to the ground.

Lara jumped out of her chair and put her hand on Mozer's shoulder, whispering, "Your Highness, I think it's time to end the meeting."

He slowly turned to his trusted assistant and grinned with his perfect teeth flashing. "How dare you tell me what to do. Do you want to be made an example of next?"

Lara took a deep breath and retreated to her seat. Mozer bent down and pulled up Flannery by his hair.

"All of you. Find me those bloody remains. And don't you dare question or laugh, because what I say is law." Mozer unleashed another seismic slap across Flannery's face that echoed through the Great Hall. Flannery smacked the ground, face first. "Don't get up! Stay there!" Mozer returned his attention to the admirals. "You sorry saps are so lucky. I defended this kingdom from that wretched Akara! If she killed me, she'd be queen, and all of you would be dead. They'll attack again, so we need to mobilize and prepare for the worst. If you're aware of any necromancer activity, you report it to me immediately, and it will be handled. And lastly, I will not open this discussion for questions. Asking questions is weak. If you can't follow my directions or listen to me, then you shouldn't be an admiral. I think I've made the objective quite clear. Now, go, all of you."

The admirals stood up, and Lara escorted them to the door, but one took his time rising from the table.

"Get out, now!" Mozer scolded, but the man stood tall in front of the king.

"I just wanted to make sure Flannery wasn't forgotten about. He and I are in the same carriage," the admiral said.

"What's your name?"

"Admiral Holtmeyer, serving the outpost at Lostonia."

Mozer took a step closer to Holtmeyer, and Mozer's lips curved up. His eyes scanned Holtmeyer's body up and down. "I like you. You have some honor." Mozer turned around and used the cane resting on the table to poke the back of Flannery's head. "Come on, get up, and get the vlark out of my sight."

Flannery scrambled up and joined Holtmeyer's side. The two of them followed the rest of the admirals out of the Great Hall. Mozer stood there by himself and grinned. He admired his cane with the crystallized skull at the top and then chugged the mead that still rested on the table. He drank the other goblets that went unfinished by the rest of the admirals.

1

I sat at the edge of my bed, legs bouncing at full speed. I tried to catch my breath brought upon by anxious weight on my lungs. My knuckles were swollen with a dull ache. Staring at my tiny room of stained walls, dilapidated bookshelves, and a bucket on the ground catching water only made me feel worse. *How was that possible? When at any moment I'd be subject to even more abuse by—*

"Maximilian Brian Forrester!" My mom threw the door open, slammed it shut, and scowled at me. "What do you have to say for yourself?"

"Mom, you don't understand."

"Enough of the excuses and insults!" My mom struck my face with a pulverizing slap. "You're thirteen years old now! Grown men don't make excuses; they take responsibility! Now, tell me everything that happened so that my feeble brain might understand!"

I couldn't hide the tears, and I knew that would only make it worse.

"Don't cry! Grown men don't cry either!" Another slap stung my left cheek.

"Look!" I croaked with a thick voice mixed with rage and confusion. "I'm sick and tired of getting bullied every second of every day! I'm not good at any of the disciplines at school, and I'm constantly ridiculed. I'm at the bottom of my class, and I'm trying my hardest, I really am!"

"But you decided to throttle a kid on the last day of school? They don't know if they want you back next year!"

"Well, Lyle spat at me and called me a necromancer!" I exploded.

My mom's eyes widened as if she just saw a ghost. Her voice trembled, "Now, why would he call you a horrible thing like that? Our family grew up here in Verrenna. We have no ties with the Southeast at all."

I sighed in irritation. "Lyle didn't call me a necromancer for any reason in particular. He just called me that because I'm bad at everything and don't add worth to society. We all got our results from career exams, and I did the worst in every category.

So when he spit at me, that's when I lost it and pelted him." My fists clenched. "I'm tired of being made a fool."

"Violence doesn't solve anything!"

"Then why is the Silver Army planning for war against the necromancers?"

My mom's eyes bulged. "I don't know if your father and I can handle a whole summer of you being home. I think it's time for you to go visit Uncle Leopold for a while. He might help you figure some things out. Maybe you can become a blacksmith like him."

My mom thought it would be a form of punishment, but I enjoyed my time with Uncle Leopold. A summer with him away from my lonely house and my parents sounded like a dream. With a frown, I said, "You can't be serious."

"I am, and maybe he can teach you a thing or two! I'm tired of you moping around the house, and it would drive me crazy to see you waste another summer without any opportunities!"

"That's not fair," I argued, one of my better acting performances.

"Nor is having an ungrateful child! I'm going to send him a message right this moment!" She stormed out of the room, slamming the door behind her.

Sitting on my bed, I took a deep breath, lay down, and looked up at the ceiling for a few moments, smiling. *This could be one of the best summers of my life.*

The following week, summer break began, and I took a carriage paid for by my uncle since my parents couldn't afford it. I couldn't believe he agreed to accept my stay for the summer.

Maybe I could become a blacksmith with his guidance, and then I could come back to school and finally fit in for once.

Sitting in the carriage, I admired the open view of rolling hills. We crossed over rivers on wooden bridges and passed through a couple of forests. It was a two-day trip traveling through Lavarund. I was fortunate; the sun shined over the land with a gentle breeze that cooled some of the heat.

I studied the map on the cabin ceiling. Uncle Leopold lived out near a large port town called Lostonia. He had a ranch just outside the city area. His property had a small stable with a single horse and a colossal forgery where he smithed all of his creations. His career started off as just a local blacksmith in Lostonia, but once people saw his work, he never stopped getting requests. He grew so popular that the Silver Military commissioned him to design and forge the armor for admirals, generals, and spies across Lavarund.

I wish I had a shred of his talent. Perhaps I do and just need the proper guidance?

When the carriage pulled up to his plot of land, I exited the cab and thanked the driver. She even helped me carry my belongings inside his two-story house. Uncle Leopold came outside as if he were waiting by his window for me. He beamed and waved as we approached. He still had his auburn hair and beard, but gray bled through in some patches.

"Maximilian! It's so good to see you!"

"I'm glad someone feels that way," I said.

"Now I know that's not true. There are plenty of people out there who love you. Some of them you just don't know yet." He winked, and then he handed a few gold coins to the driver.

"Oh my, surely this is a mistake?" the driver said.

"No, that's all right. Thank you for making the long trip to get my nephew. Take care now!"

The driver waved goodbye, and that's when I went inside my uncle's massive house, and he showed me the bedroom where I would be staying. It was double the size of mine back home. The dressers, desk, and bedpost sparkled from the polish on the wood.

"Thank you so much!" I hugged my uncle.

"For what?" Uncle Leopold asked.

"Letting me stay with you and showing me how to become a blacksmith."

"Well, it's not going to be all fun and games now. It will be work, hard work, and I'll teach you what I can. But there's something I must talk to you about."

"What is it?"

"Let's cook some dinner first. I bet you're starving."

Downstairs in the kitchen, Uncle Leopold was in the middle of baking a turkey in the oven. He pulled it out and uncovered a few pots with mashed potatoes, gravy, and green beans. I served myself a plate and had a cup of cranberry juice. It was exciting to drink something other than water for once. We took a seat in a dining room encased with opened windows, creating the feeling of immersion in the outdoors while having shelter. We had a view of his acres of land, filled with tall grass, flowers, and trees.

"I know that blacksmithing will be hard work, but trust me, it's much better I stay here than with my parents," I said.

"Well, my sister—er—your mom knows you're always welcome to stay with me, but it's important to grow up with your parents, though, even if they do drive you crazy." Uncle Leopold poked his food with his fork. "Anyway, I said there was something I wanted to talk to you about, and it's a bit of a delicate topic. There's no easy transition, so, what do you know about necromancers?"

I lifted my brow and thought about it for a moment in between chomps of my meal. "I guess I don't really know much about them. Everyone just calls them dirty and evil. But it's weird. I've never really seen one, so I can't say if they're really as horrible as everyone makes them out to be."

"So, you wouldn't say you have any hatred toward them?"

"No, I guess not, but it certainly seems like it's the trend, especially with this new king coming in. Mozer seems to despise them."

"Yeah, he does, doesn't he? I was hoping that there might be a different outlook on things with him coming to power, but it looks like much of the same ideology his parents held. Although, I'm afraid he might be worse." Uncle Leopold gazed out the window before looking back at me. "So, you've never met a necromancer?"

"No. There are a few witches and wizards in our town, but they can't really do anything, so no one really bothers them. Like, I've heard necromancers can raise dead animals from the ground and stuff like that." I shuddered.

Uncle Leopold chuckled. "That's true. They can raise the remains of animals. But when they come up, they're not zombies. In fact, they're obedient skeletons brought to life by magic. Did you know that necromancers can also raise up human skeletons?"

I gulped as my eyes widened. "Whoa, that's kinda freaky."

"You might think so, but it's really not as frightening as it seems."

I stopped eating for a moment. "Why are you asking all of these questions?"

"As you know, I'm a bit of a renowned blacksmith. People have always said I had the right touch, the right eye, and excellent attention to detail for armor. And I can do blades and weapons, but it's not my best, though I've certainly improved over the years. When I started, I could handle the workflow one piece at a time, no problem. My name wasn't out there yet. But when I started going to the Lostonia market to sell my armored goods there, word spread that I was a different talent, so I had a flood of requests. I didn't really know how to handle the increased workflow with my signature style, until one day, where I kept an open mind and designed a knife for a necromancer.

"This necromancer kept his identity a secret, heard of my abilities, and purchased some armor and daggers for himself to see if I could live up to the hype. Apparently, I did because we had a meeting in my smaller house at the time. He showed me how to make osseous steel and how it behaves similarly to wrought iron once it's forged. It's a special alloy made of bone and another metal found in the Southeast.

"I made that necromancer a knife, and just before he left my house, he said, 'I've noticed you're in high demand for things.' And I confirmed his theory and explained how I wanted to expand my business, but it was tough because the other blacksmiths I met just didn't have my signature touch and I didn't want to put my name on something that wasn't my caliber.

"That's when the necromancer showed me I could summon skeletons to help me with my work, and they could exhibit the same touch as I had with blacksmithing, as long as I summoned them. And thus, I went through some training, bought textbooks, and, well, I think you should come see my forgery."

We finished our dinner and went outside, walking about twenty yards to the massive wooden barn structure by his house.

"Welcome to the forgery, Maximilian." Uncle Leopold put his hand on my shoulder as he unlocked the iron door with his massive ring of black keys. Sliding it open, we stepped into a vestibule with another iron door that he unlocked and opened. We were finally inside, and my jaw dropped.

Three skeletons were standing upright and moving. One was holding a pair of large black pliers that was clutching a hunk of glowing orange metal. Another was clanging away at another piece of metal on an anvil with a mallet. The third skeleton was in the middle of inspecting a plate of armor while painting it with a liquid that appeared to be polish. I stumbled back into my uncle. He caught me.

"It's okay; they're nothing to be afraid of. I've summoned them myself," Uncle Leopold said.

The skeleton that was polishing with a brush stopped and waved. "Hello! You must be Maximilian! Your uncle here is delighted to be hosting you." The teeth on the skull curved up. "The name's Conner, in case you were wondering."

"They can talk?" I whispered to my uncle.

"They're capable of a lot: speech, movement, and smithing. Whatever you can do, they can do. And don't worry, you can go up to them and shake their hand if you'd like. They're friendly."

I couldn't believe it, so I went up to Conner and shook the boney hand.

"See? Nothing to be afraid of," my uncle said behind me, patting my back. "But I do mean this when I say this, do not tell a soul that I'm a necromancer. Do you understand?"

I nodded.

"Promise me this will be kept secret?" he said.

"Of course," I said.

"It's serious, though, because people want to know how I've been able to take on a higher volume of work. They just think I can perform at a superhuman speed, but that's obviously not the case. Without them, I wouldn't be nearly as successful."

My mind was burning with curiosity and questions. "How do you do it? I mean, how do you summon them?"

Uncle Leopold smiled. "Would you say you have more of a curiosity for necromancy than blacksmithing?"

"I don't know. I guess so. I don't know what necromancy entails. Blacksmithing we've talked about in school, and we've done some lessons, but I almost failed those."

"Mhmm." We stood there while his skeletons labored. "Why don't we talk inside?"

"What about them?" I pointed at the skeletons. "Do they just work all through the night?"

"No. If we get any travelers coming by the roads, it would look suspicious that there's smithing going on 24 hours a day. Although if I wanted them to, they could. They sink back into the ground at 8:00 PM and rise back up at the crack of dawn. Come, let's talk more inside."

Back inside Uncle Leopold's house, the sun was starting to set. Uncle Leopold put on a few logs in the fireplace and prepared some tea for the two of us. I was rooted to his red leather cushioned chair with my feet up in front of the fire. Uncle Leopold sat across from me and set down two steaming hot mugs on the table between us. My skin tingled when I saw him brandishing a knife while dropping a small pile of animal bones next to his mug.

"Don't be alarmed. The knife is the tool of the necromancer. To assemble the bones to their original place and imbue them with magic, you have to say an incantation. Which is like a poem. Then, once you get to the special line in the poem, you actually have to cut your hand."

"Cut your hand?!" I blurted.

"Yes. Part of the magic is that you must give your blood to give the bones life." His smile felt so trustworthy and warm. "But it doesn't hurt if you do it correctly. I can't explain why it doesn't hurt, except that it's all part of the magical process."

"That's kinda creepy."

Uncle Leopold chuckled. "Why don't I show you an example."

"Bones are vessels of the soul. I give my blood to bring life as toll. Rise within and become my companion. Awaken and rise, reform and mend. Become one, once again."

The tip of the knife glowed a bright white. My jaw dropped as my uncle stabbed his palm. Droplets of blood shot from his wrist and landed on the mouse bones. The bones reconnected like a pile of magnets, and a fully formed mouse skeleton stared up at me, tilting its head.

"See, not a big deal at all." My uncle smiled.

"Can you show me how to do that? That was amazing!" I put my hand up to the mouse and pet its smooth bones.

"It's a little difficult to do summon magic, but we can start with another simpler spell tomorrow morning. Sound good?"

I bounced my head up and down.

"Wonderful. Let me show you something." Uncle Leopold stood up, went to another room, and returned with an old, tattered textbook in his hand. "This is the book that taught me a lot in the beginning, and I think it will be useful to you." He thumbed through the first few pages and landed on an entry. "Here's what I'd like to show you how to do first."

I took the book from him and read the heading: *Chapter 4—Bone Flowers*.

"Where did you get this book?" I asked.

"Sometimes, cities have bookstores with a special hidden section where they sell illegal texts pertaining to necromancers. This is an introductory guide to all things necromancy. You'll notice that the pages I've skipped go over some of the history the necromancers believe in. Or at least, I think some believe in it. Probably not so much anymore. To be honest, I'm not all that sure because it reads like mythology."

I skimmed the previous chunk of pages. "Huh, that's pretty fascinating. I think I might read about that stuff too."

"If you're interested, go for it. But read about that spell, and we'll work on it tomorrow."

I gulped. "Do I have to cut my hand?"

"Just read the text, and you'll find everything you need to know." Uncle Leopold smiled.

I began reading.

The summoning spell. Arguably the necromancer's most remarkable and most useful spell, it's used every day and can be applied to almost all facets of life.

This is the first summoning spell every beginner necromancer should learn. It's a simple introduction that establishes a firm base and understanding. It also doesn't require a knife or any blood, which is usually an integral part of the process.

The incantation should be said aloud. As you study and get more comfortable with it, you can whisper it. For advanced learners with a lot of training, try saying it in your mind. It takes a lot of practice and great concentration, so don't give up if you can't do it after numerous attempts. It can be mastered with patience. Memorize the following lines:

"Beneath the soil I call upon the underworld. Roots, stems, and leaves come out untwirled. Show me an ivory succulent or flower. With the earth, I'm one with your power."

You cannot read it from the text. It must be memorized perfectly in your head. Success is more likely when the incantation is spoken at a tempo of 104 beats per second, although flexibility exists. With more advanced spells and larger skeletal summons, rhythms are crucial to success.

I spent the rest of the evening memorizing the incantation. It wasn't very long, but remembering anything was always a challenge for me. My uncle and I sat there, drinking our tea, relaxing by the warm fireplace embers. I practiced reading from the text as Uncle Leopold tapped the rhythm on his thigh.

"I can't wait to try this tomorrow. This is so fascinating!" I beamed.

"Good, we'll do it first thing in the morning," Uncle Leopold said.

"Don't you have to smith?"

"The skeletons will take care of the morning load, no problem. Besides, if I could show you something that you'll love, then it is all worthwhile. Life is all about opening doors and finding out which ones you want to keep traveling through."

"Great, well, I'm gonna head off to bed then. Do you mind if I keep on reading this book before I fall asleep?"

"Not at all." Uncle Leopold hugged me goodnight, and I scooted off to bed.

By my mattress, a lantern emitted a soft glow in the room as I read the book's earlier pages. My eyes kept closing, and the words continued to blur. The terms didn't make a whole lot of sense. Images of the formation of Earth by two spirits filled my mind. This spirit was called the 'Zevolra,' *Yes? Or something like that?* And then there's this other one that was the 'Vyrux', *I think?* The lantern died out, and within seconds I fell asleep.

In the morning, I gobbled my breakfast of eggs and bacon with Uncle Leopold, and then I rushed out to the backyard. Uncle Leopold laughed as he came outside a few moments later, smiling once he saw me with my hands outstretched at the ground.

"Are you ready?" I asked.

"Are you sure you're ready?" Uncle Leopold said.

I bobbed my head up and down.

"You have it all memorized?"

I nodded. I had been reciting the whole passage in my head during our breakfast.

"All right, let's see you work your magic." He took a step back.

"Beneath the soil I call upon the underworld. Roots, stems, and leaves come out untwirled. Show me an ivory succulent or flower. With the earth, I'm one with your power."

Nothing happened.

"Say it louder," Uncle Leopold said.

Again, I repeated the incantation with extra decibels.

Nothing grew from the ground.

"Clear your mind. You're too focused on the words. Really focus, really picture the bones coming up from the earth."

All I imagined was a tulip of pure ivory, emerging from the green grass. Its texture, its glisten from the sun, its gentle dance side-to-side in the wind. I repeated the incantation again, my voice booming with my diaphragm's help.

"Hello?" a voice called out.

I jumped. *Would the plant be able to talk?*

Uncle Leopold's eyes darted to woods that made up the frame of his backyard. His mouth fell ajar. A man approached the back of the house, waving as he carried a burlap backpack wearing a wicker disc on top of his head.

"Hello? What's with all the yelling?" The man chuckled, getting closer, then he froze. "Wait a second."

I was squinting at the traveler until a white crown poked into my eyesight. I gasped. A three-foot tulip with a base of white leaves stood in front of me. "Wow." I rubbed the leaves in between my fingers and felt the stem. Smooth, dense, and pristine.

"Unsummon!" Uncle Leopold whispered.

The tulip burst into a cloud of dust that settled on the grass. I fixed my attention back on the traveler, and he gaped at the ground.

"Hello? Can I help you, sir?" Uncle Leopold strode up to him, and I followed, but my uncle whipped his head around and whispered to me, *"Stay back."*

My heart sped up, and I couldn't help but frown. Uncle Leopold had a twinge of anger in his eye. I cupped my ear towards them and inched my way closer, sliding through the grass.

"Uh hi, sorry to come upon you like this, I, uh, haven't been here before, and I got a little turned around. I'm uh, well, I was looking for a Mr. Leopold Smith?"

"Yes, that's me. How can I help you, sir?"

"Oh uh, well, n-nevermind then, ca-carry on."

"No, please, explain. A stranger enters my backyard looking for me. I deserve to know."

"I'm j-just traveling from the other side of Lavarund." He took a deep breath. "It's been a long journey, but I'm h-here to request a set of armor to be made for my s-son. It's my understanding you're the b-best in the country."

"Uh yeah, so they say. I'd be happy to help you. While I only take requests at my office in Lostonia, I will take your request under the agreement you forget everything you've seen here today. Do you understand me?"

"Su-sure." The stranger trembled.

"Let's go inside my house. I'll fix you up some breakfast; you must be exhausted." Uncle Leopold turned around, leading him to the house. I jogged back quietly.

"That's okay, si-sir. I don't need any food," the man replied.

"All right, at least have some coffee then, and we'll work up a contract for you to get your son some of the finest plates in Lavarund. Please, I'm happy to help."

They sat inside the dining room, and I sat outside, holding my ear as close to the door as possible.

"Now, look, I'm happy to do this project for you. It seems rather simple. You came prepared and brought all of his measurements. I can't tell you enough how much I appreciate that," Uncle Leopold said.

"Well, I didn't w-want to w-waste your time," the traveler said.

"Thanks. I wish more customers were like you." Uncle Leopold paused. "I'd be happy to do this project for you, for free, if that's okay with you?"

17

"For free?" the man gasped. "I was expecting several gold coins." He laughed. "Of course, that's okay with me. How long will it take?"

"Judging by the scope of the needs, I'd say it'd take around 24 hours."

"24 hours! Why, that's incredible!"

"Yes, but it's all under one condition."

Silence sat between them for an uncomfortable few seconds.

"You cannot tell a soul what you witnessed here today."

"Oh uh, s-sure."

"You can pick it up at my office tomorrow morning in Lostonia. I won't be there, but my assistant will help you."

"Great, uh, I'll be staying in Lostonia this evening then. Th-thanks."

They shook hands, and I slipped away upstairs without a sound as Uncle Leopold showed him the door. I gazed down from the staircase at the man. He said goodbye with a feigned smile.

Uncle Leopold sprinted to the forgery and didn't say a word to me other than, "Stay inside the house today. I'm sorry."

The only thing I wanted to do was practice summoning ivory flowers to see how tall I could get them, but I had to listen to my uncle. For the rest of the afternoon, I read about the necromancers from the textbook. I couldn't believe they used to live among people in the cities all over Lavarund. Nowadays, they lived in the southeast lands of Lavarund. It saddened me to find out they had been exiled by monarchs for the past few generations. When Uncle Leopold came back in the house, I said, "I had no idea about this history with the necromancers. They don't teach us this stuff in school. They're barely mentioned in history, if at all."

He entered the kitchen and fixed himself a tall glass of water from a barrel. Uncle Leopold nodded, but his signature smile was nowhere to be found. His lips were flat, and his eyes were exhausted, not from lack of sleep, but from stress. "Yes," he finally said after a lengthy pause. "The past hasn't been kind to them, unfortunately. And as you now know, anyone can be a necromancer, Maximilian." He moped into the living room and fell into the chair by the silent fireplace, rubbing his forehead. "Come here for a moment, Maximilian."

I sat on the chair opposite of him. "You okay, Uncle Leopold?"

His lips sank on both ends. "I'm going, to be honest with you, I don't know."

Silence lingered.

"Sometimes it helps me if I talk about what's on my mind," I said.

He smiled just the slightest bit. "Thank you, Maximilian. You're a good kid, you know that?"

Compliments were foreign to my ears. How does one respond to such a thing?

"And I know things haven't been very fair to you," Uncle Leopold continued, "but that doesn't mean there aren't better days to come. I wasn't able to give you credit earlier, but you summoned up an incredible ivory flower. Are you sure you've never done that before?"

I nodded.

"I'm so impressed. If that is something you want to pursue, you should. You ever think about moving away?"

I chuckled. "I think about leaving my house all the time. I wanna be as far away from my parents as possible." I thought my response would lighten the tone, but Uncle Leopold stared off into space.

"Something might happen to me, Maximilian. And it might happen during your stay here, and if it does, I want you to run. Take my horse and start a new life somewhere else. Sell the horse if you have to. You're still young, but I think you'll get by."

My eyes widened. "That sounds like crazy talk."

"It's not crazy, as much as I'd like to admit it. That man that came in here, I don't trust him at all."

"I don't know, Uncle Leopold, you said you'd give him free armor. I don't think you have anything to worry about."

He glared at me. "Were you listening in on our conversation?"

I frowned and slowly nodded.

"Dammit, Maximilian," he raised his voice. "That was wrong of you. You shouldn't have done something like that."

"I'm sorry." I got up from the seat and couldn't bear to look him in the eye. "I'll be up in my room. Let me know if you need my help for dinner or something. Again, I'm really sorry." I went up the steps, closed the door, and sat on my bed, crying into my pillow.

A few minutes later, there was a gentle knock at my door.

I picked my head up. "Y-Yeah?" I sniffled.

Uncle Leopold came into the room. "I'm sorry, Maximilian. I'm just a little on edge. This is a stressful time for me, and I didn't mean to take it out on you."

Sitting up on the bed, I continued to look at him.

"Can I have a hug?" he asked.

I nodded and leaped off the bed to wrap my arms around him. He held me for a long moment, rubbing my back.

"Let's get started with dinner, shall we?" he said.

We prepared a baked ham, potatoes, and string beans. We both had a glass of fresh grape juice and enjoyed a quiet dinner. Near the end of our meal, Uncle Leopold said, "I'm sorry, Maximilian, but as I think about everything that transpired this morning, it might be best if we didn't perform any more acts of necromancy in the backyard. I hope you understand."

The excitement I had about exploring the necromancy book deeper and continuing to practice flower summoning collapsed. I had recovered my smile when I helped Uncle Leopold with dinner, but it vanished once again.

"I know, you seem really excited about it, and I wish things were different. But please, do you understand?" Uncle Leopold asked.

"Yes, I do." I hung my head and finished off the rest of my dinner in silence.

The following day, Uncle Leopold finished the requested armor. He delivered it to his office in Lostonia, which only took him an hour riding his horse in and out. He even took that moment to introduce me to his horse, Betty. She was tall with black and white spots, like a cow. I petted her nape, and she responded by licking my hand, coating it with slimy saliva.

"Yuck." I flicked the saliva off my hand.

Uncle Leopold chuckled, which was nice to hear. "Don't worry, Maximilian, she likes you. Glad you two have met."

"She's such a friendly horse." I admired her giant brown eyes.

"We have a few minutes still. Why don't you hop on and take her for a little ride around the fence?"

"Uh, sure." I hopped on her back and rode around the circumference of the enclosed space. My body trembled as we started to move, but she galloped at a gentle pace. After a couple minutes, I was relaxed. "She moves kinda slow," I called out to my uncle.

He laughed. "Trust me, she can go a lot faster than that. There's no need to right now, though. Just wanted you to be acquainted. Also, before I leave, here's a key to the stable. Keep it in your bedroom or something."

I slid off Betty and took the key from his hand. He hopped on the horse.

"I won't be gone long, so just stay in the house and don't answer the door for anyone. And watch me take off; you'll see some of Betty's speed here." Uncle Leopold winked, and then the horse bulleted from the yard to the road. He wasn't kidding. She sped off like a bolt of lightning.

When Uncle Leopold came back, he spent the rest of the day in the forgery while I continued to read the necromancy book. We cooked dinner again like the night before. The rest of the evening was spent enjoying tea in front of the fire. Uncle Leopold's lips were curved up the whole time.

"I think I'm going to head off to bed; I'm getting tired." I yawned.

"Why don't you wait right here a quick moment? There's something I'd like to give you." He went upstairs and came back down within a few seconds. He handed me a burlap sack that fit in my hand.

"What's this?" I asked.

"In case anything happens, like an emergency. No, no, please don't open it in front of me. I only want you to open it if there's trouble of any kind."

"What kind of trouble?"

"You'll know." His eyes narrowed. "No need to thank me or mention it again; just take the bag, as well as this." He handed me a knife that was sheathed in a leather case. The handle was designed with shiny ivory. The guard felt resilient, like a durable bone, and the pommel at the bottom had the shape and design of an ivory snake eye.

"What's this?"

"It's my necromancy knife. I have another one I made for myself, but it's my finest one I've made. I want you to keep it in your room. Like I said, if anything happens, it's yours."

"Thank you, a lot. I feel bad taking this. Are you sure?"

"Don't feel bad, and yes, I want you to have it. You can head off to bed now." He took a deep breath.

"Okay. Goodnight, Uncle Leopold," I said.

"Goodnight, Maximilian," he said, and just as I turned the corner to head up the stairs, he added, "I love you, nephew."

"I love you, too."

Admiral Holtmeyer marched to the docked boat at the Silver Navy base. It was going to be another long night of exploration on the Bolt Sea. Holtmeyer felt he didn't need to be there. His crew, who was waiting for him on the ship, had shown they could follow the instructions. Holtmeyer would have let them go alone, but he wasn't sure how anyone would react if they found something of significance. A lot of them got drunk off booze and could get boisterous on occasion. As much as he wanted to stay at the outpost and fall asleep, he knew he had to be there. He had given commands of the outpost to his assistant, Royce, who was sprinting after him on the docks in the dark.

Holtmeyer spun around. "What is it, Royce?"

"Admiral Holtmeyer, I believe we have a serious situation that requires your immediate attention."

"What have you heard?"

"Well, a member of the Silver Army that's stationed in Lostonia received word two days ago that someone rather important is a necromancer." Royce shuddered.

"Who might that be?"

"Leopold Smith."

Holtmeyer blinked. "You're kidding."

"No, sir. A traveler who was at Smith's ranch two days ago said Smith was out there summoning up something bad with his son."

Holtmeyer turned around and continued towards the ship. "He doesn't have a son. Sounds like a rumor to me."

"No, no, no, it's serious. The traveler said that he saw Smith with a kid, and then Smith offered to give him free armor if he kept his mouth shut. Then it gets worse. I wouldn't waste your time if it was just the one off-handed account. A Silver Spy watched his house all day and night yesterday. The spy said that it sounded like many people were working inside the forgery, even though no one ever came in or out except Smith. Smith didn't bring in any food or water either. I gotta say, as much as I hate to admit it, I always wondered about how Smith did things so fast, and it makes sense if he's using skeletons to do this work."

"Huh." Holtmeyer sighed. "This is troubling. I rather liked Leopold. He's a good man."

"I know, and to find out he's a traitor is just baffling. Smith is a true Lavarund hero. Or, at least he was." Royce hung his head.

"Yeah, I don't know, sounds like a rumor to me, but if the Silver Army Spy confirms what he heard and saw, then, damn. Sounds like we have to do something about it."

"Which is why I told you. You're the highest-ranking official in this region. From what I understand, it's up to you to—"

"Yes, yes, I'm aware of the procedures and protocols." Holtmeyer heaved a deep breath. He was somewhat relieved he wouldn't have to get on the ship tonight, but he didn't like what had to be done.

"What do you want to do with tonight's reconnaissance?" Royce asked.

"Why don't you take over? And I'll give some other bloke command of the outpost tonight."

"Are you sure about that? I don't even know what we're supposed to be looking for or what to do if we find anything."

Holtmeyer pulled out his expanded map of the Bolt Sea and pointed to a circled section. "Send down some nets and the treasure claw in this region. Once the sun comes up and trade boats start returning, come back to the docks."

"What am I looking for? Gold? Gems?"

"You're looking for bones. Giant remains of something. Allegedly, there is a weapon deep in the waters of Lavarund that the necromancers are after. So, watch out also for any necromancer ships, not that I ever see any, but they might be out there."

"Got it."

"I'll see you later, thank you." Holtmeyer patted Royce's back and went to the stables of the outpost. He received a few concerned glances from the night guards, but they didn't say anything. "I'll be back later this morning," Holtmeyer told them. As he got in a double horse carriage and left the outpost, whisperings broke out among the guards.

Traveling through the night wasn't Holtmeyer's favorite. Still, he had stayed up enough during the sea explorations that he didn't feel tired, though he would have welcomed rest. The two horses didn't gallop fast. It was dark, even under the stars and bright moon. All he had was a dangling lantern on the cab to give them a modest radius of light.

After several hours of travel, he came up to the Lavarund Royal Castle front gate, guarded by an operator in a turret and two Silver Army guards at the top.

"Please state your business," the operator in front of the moat said.

"I'm Admiral James Holtmeyer from Lostonia," he stated.

"May I see some identification?"

"Sure thing." Holtmeyer pulled out a silver amulet containing an aquamarine gem from inside his breastplate.

The operator observed it with a magnifying glass. He handed it back to Holtmeyer. "Very good, come on through."

The giant wooden drawbridge clanked down until it connected with the land. The three-story castle with a purple roof, four corner turrets, and a center spire of stone towered over Holtmeyer. He secured his identification amulet in his armor and took a moment to appreciate what he was wearing. *Vlark it all. Why'd it have to be him?* he thought.

His horses galloped ahead to the castle until he made it inside the stables, which was also overseen by another guard that Holtmeyer had to show his identification to. If he were a lower rank, he'd have to be escorted by someone from the Silver Army.

Inside the castle walls, he strolled through the flagstone corridors all the way to Lara's room and knocked on her arched iron door on the third floor. On his trek through, he barely saw any servants or guards. *They must all be on watch in the turrets,* he thought.

"Mozer, is that you?" Lara asked through the door.

"No, it's Admiral Holtmeyer from Lostonia."

The door swung open. Her brow raised as she stared at him. "What time is it? What happened?" Lara ushered him inside and closed the door behind her. She turned on a lantern by her bed. Holtmeyer observed how empty the room was and thought about commenting on it, but decided it wasn't the time or place. "This must be pretty serious," Lara said.

"Yeah, uh." Holtmeyer lost his train of thought. He'd never seen Lara in a nightgown. Conversations always had the utmost formality. "I received some horrible news. A high-profile Lavarund citizen is a necromancer."

Lara's jaw dropped. "Who is it?"

"Leopold Smith. The very same man that creates the armor for high-ranking Silver Military members."

She stared at the ground and exhaled a deep sigh. "Are you sure?" Her head twitched from side to side. "Of course you're sure. Otherwise, you wouldn't be here right now."

Holtmeyer nodded.

"Uh, why don't you go see the king and deliver the news to him?" Lara asked.

"I don't even know where his room is."

"It's just further down the hall. You'll go through another set of doors and continue straight down. Can't miss it. Knock on his door when you get there."

"What if he doesn't answer? Shouldn't he be sleeping?"

"Come back to my room, and I'll get him."

Holtmeyer nodded and followed the corridor until he reached the end, to a set of arched double black doors. He knocked on the metal, but there was no reply. He banged his fist, unsure of what else to do, and then the door cracked open.

"Yes?" a woman's voice whispered. Holtmeyer could barely see her face.

"Hello. I'm sorry to disturb you so late in the evening, but I'm Admiral Holtmeyer from Lostonia. I've come to deliver a message to King Mozer, and I've already received permission from his assistant."

"He's not in the room currently," she said and slammed the door.

Holtmeyer had no idea who that was. There was no official queen of Lavarund. *Perhaps that woman would become queen?* Holtmeyer thought, but he knew better than to ask. He went back to Lara's room, and just before he went in, he could hear sniffling on the other side of the door.

Lara answered, fully dressed in clothes more suitable for combat practice. Tight clothing with no armored plates. "Was he not in his room?"

Holtmeyer observed her tired eyes. Her face glistened with tears. "No, I'm afraid he wasn't. A woman answered and told me he wasn't in."

"Vlark. Okay, follow me then." Lara hurried ahead, and Holtmeyer followed behind. They traveled through the castle, coming to a hall that stretched on for many yards in the basement. There was only one door all the way at the end, and echoed yells grew louder the closer Holtmeyer and Lara approached.

Holtmeyer's blood ran cold as he heard a drawn-out, anguished bellow coming from a man. "Lara, what's happening down here?"

Lara sighed. "I wish I knew."

Another tormented moan made the hairs on Holtmeyer's neck stand up.

"Or maybe it's better I don't know," Lara said hopelessly.

They came up to an arched iron entrance, and Lara punched it several times with the side of her fist. Her knock overpowered the periodic screaming.

After a few seconds, the door split open, and Mozer jumped out, slamming it shut behind him. Holtmeyer and Lara didn't see a thing. Mozer glared at the two of them, only wearing pants with some dried blood on his chest and face. "You interrupted me?"

He stepped up to Holtmeyer, inches away from his face. His voice was close to a whisper. "What's your name?"

"Admiral Holtmeyer from the outpost in Lostonia. We've met before."

Mozer's eye twitched, and his lips curved up. "Shouldn't you be out on an expedition this evening on the Bolt Sea?"

"More pressing matters came up," Holtmeyer said, holding himself with perfect posture. "Leopold Smith is a necromancer."

"Please! Help me," a man cried through the wall. "I don't know anything about spies. If you can hear me, please!"

Mozer didn't react to the outburst, but he grinned at Holtmeyer. "Sounds like we have some work to do."

"According to procedures, I am to lead the imprisonment operation against him, correct?" Holtmeyer asked.

"Nah. That's not going to happen. Things are different around here now. You won't have to worry about a single thing. Just let me take care of it. After all, to be a good king, I must take care of my people." Mozer put his arm around Holtmeyer's shoulder, dragging his hand around Holtmeyer's nape and up to his face. He caressed Holtmeyer's cheek. "Thank you for delivering this information to me."

Holtmeyer wanted to back away, but his spine froze up. Lara stared at the scene, trying to disguise her frown.

"What are you going to do about Smith?" Holtmeyer asked.

Mozer stared into his soul. "Don't worry about it. You've got some nerve to ask, though. But I like that; you're gutsy."

Holtmeyer's skin crawled.

"Lara, prepare some men for tomorrow evening. Looks like we're making a trip to our friend, Leopold." Mozer smirked. "Now, get the vlark away from me."

Lara and Holtmeyer paced out of the hall, but the entire time, Holtmeyer could feel Mozer's eyes piercing his back as he walked away. He thought about turning around, but he knew the wide-eyed glare from Mozer would give him nightmares.

7

In the middle of the night, a thunderous crack came from downstairs. I sat up, whipping my head towards the door. My heart rattled, and I couldn't catch my breath. My blood ran cold as the doorknob slowly turned and the door opened. Just as I was about to scream, I saw Uncle Leopold's face. He held his hand up to me.

"I'll be right back. Stay up here," he whispered, then tiptoed downstairs.

I slid over to the ajar door with my ear cupped against the wood. Glass was breaking wood was smashing. My uncle's words echoed in my head, but I wanted to investigate with him and—

"Ahhh!" my uncle screamed, which was followed by a slapping sound and a cacophony of plated footsteps. Tears spilled from the corner of my eyes. A thump shook the floor.

"What are you doing here?" my uncle yelled.

"Don't raise your voice to me!" Another smack rang through the house. "Don't you know who I am?!"

"I'm sorry, Your Highness!" Uncle Leopold shouted. "But please, tell me what I've done wrong, for I don't know!"

Slow laughter built up into a cackling shriek. "It all makes sense now. You've been using necromancy to pump out all that work. It's a shame. I was an admirer for the longest time. Looks like your prices are gonna shoot up in value."

I grabbed the sack and knife from my drawer.

"No!" I yelped, racing down the steps into the living room. Members of the Silver Army lined the walls, clutching their poleaxes at their sides, staring forward. King Mozer gripped my uncle's hair while he was on his knees. Uncle Leopold's face was covered in crimson.

King Mozer beamed at me with a sadistic, crooked grin. "Oh? And who might this be?" he said with a slithery voice.

"Vlark you!" Uncle Leopold cursed. "It's me you want. Leave him out of this! Go, run!"

"Or stay!" King Mozer shouted, still staring at me with chilling blue eyes that pierced my soul. "He looks like the perfect age to witness death for the first time. You know, I was younger than him when I witnessed my first live killing—eight years old. I watched a member from the Silver Army slice up a necromancer." King Mozer ripped out a short sword from the top of his cane and chuckled. "It's fun when history repeats itself."

"Run now! Get out of here!" Uncle Leopold shouted over tears that raced out of his eyes.

I sprinted towards the back of the house, and the Silver Army chased after me.

"Halt! I give the vlarking orders around here, last I checked! I didn't tell you to chase after him!" Mozer hollered.

The Silver Army stopped and returned to the living room.

As I bolted out through the back of the house, powered by adrenaline, I heard King Mozer order from the living room, "Let him go! He carries enough shame! When he thinks back on his sadness, he'll realize that it was necromancy that robbed him of his family, and when he's older, he'll thank me for what I did!"

I ran to the stable, jammed the key in the gate, and got Betty out. I hopped on her back, and we shot off into the night. My heart drummed, sweat poured, and tears streamed. I had no idea where I was going or what I was doing; I just kept riding south at full speed. The thought of going to my parents' house crossed my mind, and that was the default plan, but it made my stomach tie in knots.

What would I tell my parents? What would my mom think of her brother if I told the truth? They seemed so happy to kick me out of the house.

Betty continued to gallop through the night. I wasn't tired in the slightest, even though I thought I'd need some sleep. Following the roads, we traveled to the southeast of Lavarund. It was the only decision that made sense.

When the sun rose and hovered over the horizon, exhaustion hit me like a hammer. I pulled Betty off the trail to a campsite where travelers were coming and going. All eyes were on me. I was by far the youngest one there, but I didn't feel uncomfortable. The two Silver Army guards standing by two horses didn't pay much attention to me, but just the sight of them and their red emblem on their plates, the Lavarund flag (which was the symbol of fire), made my heart sink.

I tied up Betty to a post and gazed at a map. Grayed-out was the southeast region, shaped in a dog-leg in the middle of the Poro Sea, but they left the two major cities labeled. Orbavue was one of them, which was slightly south of the official border. It was a major port center for the Poro Sea. I remember reading that it had a population of 60% Necromancers, 30% witches, and 10% humans. The city that was calling my name was Nezura. A society with 95% Necromancers and 5% witches. It was located at the end of the dog-leg, practically on the opposite side of Orbavue.

My lips pulled up on both sides while my eyelids sank. "Be back soon," I whispered to Betty and rubbed the side of her neck. Trudging deep into the campsite, I found a patch of dirt tucked away with the help of trees. I collapsed to the ground, and my eyes closed without my control.

I was in my bedroom at my uncle's house, and a bright light shined through the window. Birds chirped songs to each other outside. The smell of bacon greeted my nose, and just as I got out of bed, Uncle Leopold came inside.

"Uncle Leopold!" I raced over to him and squeezed him with a crushing hug.

"Maximilian," he said gently.

"I had a horrible nightmare."

"I'm sorry, Maximilian."

"Huh?" I could feel Uncle Leopold fade in my arms.

"I can't stay any longer. I wish I could."

"No!" I shrieked. "What do you mean? You just came into my room."

"Yes, but it's time for me to go."

"Why are you leaving?"

"You'll be fine. Trust your gut. Whatever you do, you won't be wrong."

"What? Why are you saying this?"

"Goodbye. I'm terribly sorry for everything. I did what I thought was best. Please, find it in your heart to forgive me."

"Uncle Leopold! You can't leave; I need you! You did nothing wrong!" My arms tightened around him as I cried, but he faded into nothing. It was just me, alone in the room. The light from the window brightened, making me squint.

The blinding sun burned my eyelids. A sadness lingered like a viral infection. I woke up, gripped my shirt, and felt my arms. My lungs trembled. *This is real.* Rubbing my eyes with my knuckles, I cleared away some tears. It took me a moment to realize where I was and what I had been doing. I took the bag off my back and checked to make sure no one was around.

What did my uncle leave me with?

I had my knife, which was in pristine condition, and I pulled open the small bag. For a moment, I thought it may have been a weapon or a charm. But his gift made me cry.

A pouch full of gold coins.

I couldn't believe my eyes. I'd never seen so much money before in my life; there had to be at least fifty gold coins in there. I felt the smooth metallic medallions.

My stomach roared. This lingering ache left me hungry yet void of an appetite at the same time. I jogged back to the posts where the travelers had tied up their horses. There were only a dozen of them parked, and not a single one was Betty. I must've looked them up and down a thousand times, but no, it was true. Betty was gone.

I screamed with every ounce of air in my lungs.

I circled around the campsite, hollering, "Betty! Betty! Betty!" but there was no reply. Not a single horse perked their ears.

I trudged back to the map and studied how much ground I still had to cover. Judging by the sun's distance, it was early in the afternoon. *I could probably make it to Orbavue late in the evening and maybe sleep in a park or something.* I sprinted away from the map and continued down the path to the Southeast.

During my run, there was nothing but farmland and rolling hills. The sun was setting on the horizon, and I was finally getting close to the Southeast border, but I had to cross through the Orbavue Forest. Coming up to it, the sun had descended completely. My knees wobbled with each step, my stomach felt like it shrank in size, and I was parched. My heels and shoulders weighed a thousand pounds.

Entering the forest, I just wanted to collapse on the grass and fall asleep again, but I forced myself to keep going. It helped that I had never seen trees like the ones in the Orbavue Forest. Tall pines with purple needles. Each one took up twice the size of a regular full-grown pine. There were so many trees they blocked out the light, making my surroundings much darker as the sun still gifted the sky an indirect shine. My skin tingled, the air was colder, and a fog formed around me, thickening with every second. The owls and crickets performed their nightly symphony, which I didn't mind, but I shivered when I heard a howl echo from the forest. The adrenaline that kicked in sped up my legs along the path. *Did the howl come from behind me or in front of me?*

There was something else that made my skin crawl. Pairs of round blue lights blinked at me from the trees and through the fog. I had no idea what I was looking at, but the lights followed me like a set of pupils.

Another howl shook me to my core. I stopped and scanned my surroundings, trying to peer through the fog. Any tiredness I had earlier was gone. I was wide awake, ready to take flight.

Dead leaves crunched all around me on the path. Shadowy figures dashed around in a circle, and I saw a gleam from their yellow eyes. There were multiple of them. I could hear their snarling breaths grow closer. I trembled, my chest tightening up. There was no way I could outrun them; they had me cornered.

Suddenly, a fast-paced trotting came behind me. The creatures fled in the opposite direction as a glow from a lantern drowned me in light. I squinted, my eyes still adjusting.

"What's a boy like you doing in the Orbavue Forest at night?" the woman asked sharply.

I was about to respond, but then my jaw dropped. I was standing in front of a skeletal horse attached to a carriage made of bones.

The woman shook the lantern at me. "Excuse me, boy, are you all right? Are you lost?"

"I, uh, I don't know," I uttered, my body quivering.

"My goodness, you seem ill. Here, come with me." She helped me onto the bench where she held the reins to the horse. "Don't you know you have to be very careful when you come into the Orbavue Forest at night? Dire wolves run wild and attack anyone that isn't carrying a light with them. You're lucky I found you in time." She grabbed onto the reins and flicked her wrist; the horse galloped ahead, running as fast as an average stallion.

"Thank you for picking me up and saving my life back there," I finally said, rubbing my arms to warm them up.

"Where are you traveling to?"

"I don't know, I think Nezura."

"What do you mean 'you think?' You don't know?"

"A lot's happened in the last 24 hours." I sighed. "I grew up in Verrenna. Just recently found out that I want to be a necromancer, and I can't go back to my family."

"Ah yes." The woman nodded. "A runaway. I know things may seem bleak now, but you're making a decision you won't regret. Living as a necromancer is a wonderful life, despite what you might have heard from the mainland. My name is Megan, nice to meet you," she said. With one hand still on the reins, she shook my hand.

"My name is Maximilian. Nice to meet you, too. If you don't mind me asking, where are you heading?"

Megan chuckled. "Of course I don't mind you asking. I'm heading to Nezura. Just stopped off at a farm to pick up some pumpkins. Got held up talking to the farmer and even had dinner. Anyway, I can take you to Nezura if that sounds good to you?"

"Uh, sure, how much would that cost? I have some money."

Megan cracked up. "You're a good kid with some good manners. Look, I have no problem taking you into Nezura, free of charge. I was heading there anyway, and so far, you've been nothing but good company to me. It's my pleasure."

"Thank you so much." My stomach followed up with a loud growl.

"Are you hungry?" Megan gave me a side-eye.

"Uh, yes."

"Why didn't you say anything earlier?" She reached behind her back and pulled out an ivory basket with a closed lid. She handed it to me. "Knock yourself out. There are some necromancer dumplings in there. Don't worry, they're not made of bones or dead things. It's a wonderful vegetarian soup dish."

"How many can I have?" I opened the lid and marveled at the food like a chest full of treasure.

"You're going to kill me with your kindness. Have as many as you want. Please eat them all, I mean it too. They're delicious, made them myself."

"You sure?" I asked, but she replied with a glare.

I fit a whole one in my mouth, and upon the first bite, it exploded with warm broth and crisp vegetables. Pepper, garlic, and a variety of other flavors danced on my tongue. I was more awake, alert, and revitalized. I ate another, and another. "These are wonderful!"

"Glad you like them." She smiled.

I devoured all ten of them. "Thank you so much!"

"My pleasure."

"By the way, what are all of those pairs of blue lights that are glowing everywhere? I find them unsettling."

"Don't we all? They're Marruts. Small mammals that live in trees with eyes that emit blue light through the forest. Pretty harmless, but they're only native to the Orbavue Forest."

"Explains why I've never seen them before."

"You'll be learning a lot about life here in the Southeast."

The skeletal horse continued to carry us through the forest at impressive speeds until we finally made it out, arriving at a vast stretch of flat land. A few farms, but many dried out fields. I saw a castle to my left on the horizon with a variety of other buildings. Their windows were aglow with soft flames from lanterns.

"That's Orbavue over there—a nice port town. I do a lot of trading back and forth between there and Nezura," Megan said.

"Who lives in the castle?"

"Oh, no one actually lives inside the castle. It's just the Municipality Building. All the town leaders have their offices there and hold meetings. In the Southeast, we're just governed by the law of our cities."

As we continued to ride through the night, the sun rose, painting the land with a pink and orange hue on the hills. There were hardly any clouds. It was going to be a beautiful, sunny day. A few more hours passed, and on the horizon, a metropolis came into view, a city built on a hill: so many buildings and places to explore. Walls of bone came up from the ground like ribs protecting the city's border. My heart kicked up with excitement and hope.

"So, you've never been to Nezura before?" Megan asked.

"No, I haven't. This is my first time in the Southeast," I said.

"Up at the very top is a park called Caster's Court. The colossal tower where you see a giant skull on top is where they make city-wide announcements, and they use it as an observation tower. I think it's mostly for show, but there is a practical use to it. It's called Skull Tower. How original, I know. And then that tall domed building you see on the left is the Municipality Building for Nezura. That's where the Noble Necromancers work."

"Noble Necromancers?"

"Yes, they're our city leaders. Elected officials, kind of; you must be recognized by one of them, and there must be an opening. There are thirteen of them."

"Wow, you're right. I do have a lot to learn."

We had to enter through town at a specific gate where no one else was waiting to get in, but a few travelers were on their way out, carried by skeletal horses in carriages.

"How are ya, Megan? Who you got with ya?" the young gatekeeper said, smiling.

"Pretty good, Vera. Just found a runaway on my way back from Blanchard's."

"Ahhh, welcome! You're pretty young, kid. You're making a good decision. First thing he's going to have to do is go to the Municipality Building." She pulled out a slip of ivory paper and handed it to Megan. She passed it over to me; it was folded but didn't wrinkle. It said: Runaway—Assign Host.

"See you later! Welcome to your new home." The gatekeeper waved. The skeletal horse proceeded through the gate, and we entered the bustling metropolis. I'd never seen so many people running down busy streets while many were lounging out in front of restaurant patios. On the corners, bards sang songs; some of them were skeletons, some were human, and some combined their efforts to form a band with a double bass, guitar, and sticks, which were drummed off the rib cages of the skeletons.

"Wow, everyone seems so merry," I observed.

"Yeah, we like to have a good time. But many people also work storefronts and a variety of other jobs. Let's take you to the Municipality Building and get you situated," Megan said.

"Where do you think I'll be staying?"

We traversed down the road of pristine gray pavement. "I don't know. The Nobles should be able to help you out with that. I'd love to offer you my place, but I already have too many roommates." She gave me a side glance with a frown.

After being silent for a moment, I said, "That's okay, I understand."

We arrived in front of a towering dome structure. Pillars, which were probably made of osseous steel, circled the building. Megan parked the horse carriage on a post, and we walked in through the front. Inside, the lobby had a vaulted ceiling; our echoed footsteps bounced off the marble walls. The scent of old books in a library filled the air.

"Technically, you're on your own now, but I'll wait with you to make sure you're not alone." Megan put her hand on my shoulder.

"Thanks," I said.

We approached the counter, and I handed my slip to the receptionist.

"Ah, yes." He glanced at the slip. "Wait here, I'll get you the Noble Necromancer, Telyos. He's a busy man, but he'll talk with you in just a moment."

"Do you mind if we look around? He's never been here before?" Megan asked.

"Uh, you're technically not supposed to, but go for it. Just stick to the center, and I'll call you when they're ready."

Megan strolled deeper into the Municipality Building. The center had many rows of benches and a painted design of an orange monster on the ceiling. It had a unique crown of horns coming from the top of its head. Its wingspan took up the majority of the painting.

"Ah, that's the mythological being Zevolra. Said to have been partially responsible for creating our world. Some necromancers believe it as fact. Others just embrace it as part of our mythical past."

"It's pretty freaky. Ten blue eyes with insect-like pinchers." I shuddered.

Megan gasped.

"Is everything all right?" I said.

"Uh, yes. That woman on the second floor walking around the railing. That's the Noble Necromancer Akara. Come, let's get out of here. I'd hate for her to see us bending the rules."

We stepped back into the lobby. "Is she a big deal or something?"

"Well, they're all a big deal, but Akara especially, yes. I should have given you a breakdown on all of them."

I rubbed the back of my head and smirked. "Uh, that's okay. There's like thirteen of them, right? That's a lot to go over all at once."

"You'll get to know them eventually. You should know about Akara. She was anointed a few years ago and is an inspiration to us all. Started as a normal pupil in schools, but once she started teaching, she kept expanding her education, venturing into discoveries necromancers had never even dreamed of. Her imagination, dedication, and wit are not to be underestimated. She even stopped a deadly, infamous Silver Army Spy, saving the city from a ton of trouble. One of my favorite things about her is how humble she is. I've heard that if you talk with her, she focuses on your conversation and really listens."

"You've never met her?"

"No, I haven't met anyone from the current regime, really. Even though there are some old-timers, I'm not important enough for them to talk to." Megan chuckled.

"What do you know about the guy I'm about to talk to? Telyos? That was his name, right?"

"Right. Telyos is—"

"Excuse me," the receptionist interrupted. "Telyos will now accept your visit. Follow me."

"Wait." Megan grabbed my arm. "Before you leave, I just wanted to say it's been great to know you. Here, take this slip; it's my address. I can't promise I'll always be home because I'm on the road a lot, but feel free to drop by whenever you'd like. I know how hard it can be starting on your own like this."

"Thank you!" I jumped in her arms and squeezed so tightly that I thought I was never going to let go.

"Of course, it was my pleasure. Please, come visit soon, and good luck."

The receptionist took me to an office with a high ceiling. A man was sitting behind the desk, reading a document. He was tall and athletic with a sculpted face. I sat across from him, and he set down his scroll of parchment and dismissed the receptionist.

"Hello. My name is Telyos, nice to meet you."

"Nice to meet you, too. My name's Maximilian."

"So Maximilian, first I'd like to welcome you to Nezura. I'm glad you've come. Do you have any family members or friends that live here?"

"Uh, no." I frowned.

"That's all right, not a problem at all. Tell me about yourself, your background, and what led to this decision. Don't worry, this isn't a test or anything like that. You'll still have a home here, but it might not be what you'd expect."

"That's okay. I don't really know much about necromancy. I can summon a good bone flower from the ground, but that's as far as my knowledge goes. I grew up in Verrenna, and I felt like an outsider my whole life. The most exciting thing that's ever happened to me was when my uncle showed me how to create a bone flower, but then —" my voice broke at the end, and my eyes brimmed.

"That's okay, you don't have to continue. Thank you for telling me. If you'd like to talk more, I'm here for you, but I know we just met, so I don't want you to feel pressured to share anything you don't want to."

"K-King M-Mozer killed my uncle." My chest sank and ached. A wave of intense emotion burst through my head, and I sobbed.

Telyos got up from his desk and came to my side. He held my hand. "I'm sorry, Maximilian. Everything will be all right. You're here now. We'll put you in a loving home, and you'll enroll in our educational program. You'll be safe here. You're part of our family. Trust me, I was also a runaway, and my life couldn't be better."

I nodded but still had tears streaming. I stood up and gave him a hug; he wrapped his arms around me and rubbed my back. Once I pulled away, he met my eye line and took a deep breath.

"We get younger people that flee to our city for refuge regularly. You're not alone," Telyos began. "With that said, we do have a program in place that will help take care of you. Some older people in Nezura can still take care of themselves, but they could use a young person around the house to prepare them breakfast and dinner and do their chores. They aren't able to summon skeletons to help them with their daily tasks because of their age. Also, you'll earn a monthly stipend: a gold coin every four months, basically, a silver coin every month. Still, you won't have to worry about paying any landowning fees or anything like that. All supplies you could ask for will be provided by the house you'll live in."

Even though my head was exploding with raw emotions, I understood every word. I was hopeful at the prospect of living in a peaceful house, especially with a gold coin payment at that rate. I had never earned anything close to that kind of money—just a couple of coppers every two weeks for doing household chores.

"That sounds good." I wiped the tears off my face. My eyes were finally starting to dry.

"You'll be living with Mr. Cole, a dedicated necromancer his whole life. Born and raised here in Nezura. I don't know anyone who's ever had a bad thing to say about him."

I nodded.

"I'll take you to his house whenever you're ready." Telyos smiled.

Mr. Cole lived on the southern side of Nezura, where the hill sloped up, not too far from the largest park, Caster's Court. On the way to Mr. Cole's house, Telyos showed me the two-story school building that took up an entire block where I would have all my classes from 9:00 AM to 3:00 PM every weekday. Telyos also told me to get in touch with him if I ever needed his assistance.

We arrived at a narrow, two-story ivory stone building surrounded by others that looked the same. Telyos knocked on the door, and an old man using a bone-ore walker opened it. His face had deep wrinkles, and his eyes were half-closed, but he had the warmest smile and gentlest voice. "Telyos! To what do I owe this honor?"

"Good news, Mr. Cole. As a necromancer who's part of the mentor-assistance program, you now have an assistant. Fresh from the outer world of central Lavarund. Meet Maximilian."

"Nice to meet you, Maximilian. Welcome to our home." Mr. Cole shook my hand. "Please, though, call me Ray. Come on in, I'll give you a tour."

I said my goodbyes to Telyos, and Mr. Cole showed me around his house. He had a little kitchen area with a cauldron and a living room with a table and a couch. There was a door at the other end of the house and a staircase to the left. The house was much cleaner than I expected.

"This is pretty much everything," Mr. Cole said, smiling. "Your room is upstairs. Sorry if things are dusty. I haven't been up there in a while. My darn legs don't allow for much movement, as I'm sure you can imagine. But make yourself right at home. I can still cook, so, please, let me make you some dinner. There's no better way to get to know someone than sharing a meal together. Especially with my famous necromancer dumplings. Have you had those before?"

"Uh, yes, actually. I had many of them earlier today," I said.

"Ah well, let me cook you up something else. Do you have any favorite foods?"

"I really like breakfast meals, eggs, pancakes, stuff like that."

Mr. Cole grinned from ear to ear. "Please, go upstairs. You'll find your bedroom and a bathroom. Make the space your own. While you're up there, I'll get started on some eggs and pancakes. Good choice, my boy."

I walked up the steps and analyzed every nook and cranny. The house smelled of various spices. Cobwebs dominated the corners of the hall, connecting to the bedroom and bathroom. A thin layer of dust left a footprint with each step, but everything was neat and organized. My room upstairs had a large bed that could easily fit two people comfortably, along with a dresser, a bookcase, and a nightstand.

Wow, this is way better than my bedroom back at Verrenna.

I opened up the shelf of the nightstand and deposited the ivory slip that Megan gave me. I made sure to burn a concrete memory of putting it there. I even read the address repeatedly, even though I had no awareness of where Venom avenue was.

Reaching into my bag, I pulled out my knife and sack of coins and put them in the dresser as well. I wanted to ask Mr. Cole what I should do with all the money my uncle gave me, but I just met him. It seemed like a strange thing to bring up so soon. I decided it was best to wait a while.

I sat on the bed for a moment. I was impressed with how soft the mattress was, like a thick layer of foam. As I stared up at the ceiling, I smelled the batter cooking. My nose tingled, and I remembered the few happy days I had back in Verrenna when my mom would make pancakes on my birthday.

12 years later…

I had made an appointment with Telyos regarding my circumstances.

When I went to the Municipality Building, I didn't have to wait long in the lobby before the receptionist took me to the office I hadn't been to since I was thirteen. It was strange walking in there as I held a bag of gold coins.

Telyos' hair had slightly grayed, the wrinkles on his face were more pronounced, but he still looked just as sharp as when I first met him.

"Hi, Telyos, do you remember me at all? We met about twelve years ago when I came to Nezura for the first time ever, completely alone. You had me live with Mr. Cole. My name is Maximilian Forrester."

"Yes, yes, it's been a while." He shook my hand. "Sorry, I don't really remember your face much, but I remember that day, yes. How are you? How has life treated you here since then?"

"Well. It's been very complicated, and I don't want to take up too much of your time." I sighed.

"Please, don't worry about that. We can talk all day if you'd like. I care about every citizen here, and I want to make sure you're all right."

"If you insist." I rubbed my forehead, wondering where to begin. "School didn't go so well. I graduated and everything at eighteen, but I never got the hang of summoning skeletons or really any other necromancer spell. I mean, I could do well enough to pass, but, gee, I don't know. Never mastered summoning something larger than a mouse. When it came time to summon a full-body skeleton, I could get everything assembled, but it would fall apart just as it began to talk. Which was enough to pass exams, but since I've graduated, I haven't worked on my skills."

Telyos frowned. "I'm sorry to hear that. You should keep trying, though."

"But I'm twenty-five."

"That's still incredibly young. Maybe without the pressure of school and grades, you'll flourish going at your own pace."

"It's tough, though, because I'm also depressed." I paused for a lengthy moment. "I never feel like doing much of anything. Hell, it took me six months to come down here and inform you today that…Mr. Cole passed away."

Telyos' face froze. "He passed away six months ago?"

"I've cried so much I feel like I'm all cried out. I've felt emotionally drained and void of any feelings. I'm sorry it's taken me this long to tell you, but I'm asking for your understanding. I've not really been myself lately. Just been getting drunk at Risers a lot."

Telyos nodded. "I understand. You're not in trouble in any way for taking the time to inform me and making it official with the Nezura Assistance Program. We just ask you to pay back the coins you—"

I lobbed the sack of coins on his desk; it jingled as it landed on the wood.

"There are all the payments I've received since he passed. It's been a struggle, but I made it here today. I've been living off my own savings, but I'm gonna have to find a person to take care of because necromancy magic isn't my thing."

"We can help you with that, no problem." Telyos didn't even look at the bag of coins. He kept his eyes on me. "Do you own Mr. Cole's house?"

"No. He actually has a son who's in Orbavue, and he wants to sell the house. So I'm out in just a few days."

"Oh, Maximilian, I'm so sorry."

"What can you do?" I shrugged, my lips quivered, and my voice grew syrupy. "I just need a new person to take care of, if you have anyone who's looking for help."

"Yes, absolutely, but it will take me a few weeks at least to get that arranged if that's okay? Sorry, we've been rather busy here at the Municipality Building. With Akara being gone after her crusade a few years ago, things have been insane ever since. We've had an issue with Silver Spies lately, so don't forget to keep your eyes peeled."

"Honestly, take all the time you need to process. I can live on my own in a hotel for a little bit. Even mentally, I'm not sure I'm prepared to go back to helping out the older community." My eyes brimmed. Thoughts of Mr. Cole's warm smile and hugs reopened the emotional wounds.

"I understand. And that's probably best that you take time to recover. Have you thought about seeing a therapist at all?"

I sniffled. "To be honest, I haven't thought about it."

"Well, here, take this. I recommend seeing Josiah." Telyos pulled out an ivory slip from a shelf on his desk. "Stop in to his building anytime. They have a great staff of therapists who would be happy to talk to you."

I took the slip and slid it into my pocket. "Thank you, I really appreciate that."

"Absolutely. I see a therapist once a week. As you can imagine, this job is pretty stressful sometimes, especially with how things have been going the past few years." He sighed.

"Yeah, it's a good idea. I can't believe I didn't think of it sooner. I don't even have any friends I talk to or see. I was bullied all through school for never getting the hang of things." I shook my head. "I could've used therapy back then."

"That pains my heart to hear. Maximilian, I can't tell you how sorry I am."

"It's okay. Life here was all right. I know it's better than it would have been back in Verrenna. I just have to keep reminding myself of that. But I don't know, sometimes I think I'm on the edge."

Telyos' voice took a grave tone. "Edge of what?"

"Don't worry, nothing drastic. It's been an exhausting handful of years." I took a deep breath. "Well, I'd better go. I understand you're busy. I just wanted to give you this form of the official death certificate for Raymond Cole."

"Thank you, and I'm tremendously sorry for your loss. Mr. Cole was a wonderful human being."

"I know. Thankful I had him as a parent." I broke with a singular awkward laugh. "Maybe if he wasn't so easy on me, I'd be a better necromancer."

"Stop. Don't think like that. That's a dark path to go down."

"You're right, I'm sorry. Just been in a weird headspace lately. Thank you for all your help, Telyos."

"Absolutely, and Maximilian, before you leave, if you ever want to talk to me, my door is open. I know what you're going through. I took Akara's loss hard. It ripped my soul apart."

"Me too, she was a legend. The honorary mother of Nezura is what Mr. Cole and I called her."

"Yes. That's a good moniker for her. I was close to her, like a…" Telyos' lips twitched. "…like a sister to me…" His voice trailed off, and he paused before shaking his head. "Well, I'm sorry, I'm digressing. All to say, I understand how hard it is to lose someone close to you. My door is always open."

"Thanks, Telyos." I stood up to shake his hand, but he stepped around the desk and gave me a hug.

"Give some therapy a try and let me know what you think."

11

After I met with Telyos, I went to Risers, the pub that was just a few blocks from Mr. Cole's house. Inside, the tables and bar were made of ebony wood with white walls exhausted from age. There was a fireplace and never much of a crowd, an ideal environment to have an intimate conversation, or for my purpose, deep contemplation. I thought of it as my personal refuge from the busyness of Nezura.

"Hey, Max, how we doing this fine evening?" the skeleton behind the counter asked.

"Good, Henry. Could I get a glass of the melomel?" I asked.

"Absolutely, coming your way." Henry's teeth curved up as he spun around. Henry grabbed a glass and took it to a wooden keg, pumping a nozzle at the top until a cloudy amber filled the brim. He came back and dropped off the drink.

"Thank you, sir." I inhaled the fermented aroma mixed with cinnamon and blackberry. The excitement of taking a sip was the happiest I felt all day. The moment the liquid passed my lips, the sweet taste of the mead assuaged the stress and depression just a touch.

"Hey, Max, look who's here tonight." Henry pointed his boney thumb at a burly man entering through a door behind the bar. "Pub Owner King Ryoz has finally graced us with his presence." Henry's jaw clapped up and down, chuckling.

Ryoz laughed and covered his eyes. "Cmon, Henry, I told you not to call me that." He grinned. Ryoz threw a rag over his shoulder and parked his elbow on top of the bar, beaming at me. "Max, it's been a couple months, I'd say."

"How was your trip to Orbavue?" I asked.

"Good. Nice to get away once in a while. I actually went to the Lavarund National Park too. Beautiful trails, views, and wilderness. You can really relax and get away from it all deep in those woods, and even in those wide-open fields, there's not a soul around. I highly recommend camping there if you ever get a chance."

"Sounds like I should take a trip soon myself." I raised my glass to him and took a swig. "Maybe I will. Thanks for the inspiration."

"Anytime." Ryoz smiled, then studied my face. "Still haven't been feeling too well, huh?"

"I'll be okay, don't worry about me." I waved.

"If you say so. That drink is on me, by the way." Ryoz knocked on the bar and started drying glasses with his rag.

"Cheers," I said, continuing to slurp my lonely mead.

Ryoz waved and went into the back room, leaving Henry at the bar.

A wailing man came through the backdoor, his face red and wet with tears. I recognized him as I glared. He came in every once in a while, and I was thankful for his scarcity. His friend was holding him up with his arm and patting him on the back, saying, "It's all right, Rog, chin up, we're at the next pub. Pull yourself together."

I rolled my eyes and tried not to look over.

"Hey, bag of bones! My friend died! Can't I get a drink already!" the man yelled.

"Roger, they should get it to ya for free, making us wait so long," Roger's friend said.

Henry spun around and jogged up to the two of them. "Sorry, I was just on my way. What can I get for you?"

"The strongest mead you got. And whatever my friend wants," Roger blurted.

"I'll just have the house melomel," his friend said.

Henry turned back to the wooden barrels behind the bar, poured out two drinks, and delivered them. They didn't even say thank you. Henry checked on the other patrons at the tables.

"This drink should be f-free! One o' my closest friends just died, for goodness' sake!" Roger barked.

"Talk to Ryoz about that," Henry said when he came back around. "Keep it down and get your act together. Otherwise, I'm afraid I'll ask you to leave."

"Do that, and I'll cuh-rack your skuh-SKULL. I'm grievin' for cryin' out loud."

Henry's eye sockets furrowed, and he started distracting himself with other menial tasks around the bar and kegs.

"My f-friend was MUR-dered by the SIL-ver Army! A damned spuh-spy took care of 'im. Y'never know who could be a spy fer those pigs." Roger's drunken eyes wandered over in my direction. I didn't want to look, but I could feel his stare burning my face. "That guy RIGHT there, co-could be uh spy." He pointed at me. His friend also glared.

What do I do in this situation? Do I scream? Do I pull out my knife and try a necromancer spell I'm not even capable of producing? Please, someone in this bar, call this guy out!

"I seen ya around, kiddo. I ain't nu-never seen ya summon shit. Who's t'say yer not a sp-spy? It'd make sense t'me." He scowled.

"Roger, he's good. Leave him alone," Henry demanded.

"Ya can't say shit t'me! My friend d-died! Went to th' funeral t'day!" Roger roared, chugging more of his mead. He patted his friend on the shoulder. "Vlark this kid uh-up. Good-fer-nothin' spy. Preyin' on them old people, poor Mr. Cole. We all know ya. We know what yer up to." He and his friend stalked me like prey.

My heart thumped in my neck. I hadn't dealt with a physically threatening bully since I was living in Verrenna. Flashbacks paralyzed me further. My legs took root in the stool.

They leaped forward with their fists out, striking me across the face. I crashed on the ground, my head smacked the tile. They kicked me repeatedly, as hard as they could, the tips of their boots ramming into my body.

"Get the hell outta here!" someone screamed, mighty footsteps marched to my side, and the kicking stopped.

I looked up and saw Ryoz grip each man with his muscular fists and haul them outside, following it up with, "Vlark off! You're banned!" Ryoz watched them clear away before slamming the door. "Sorry about that, everyone," he said to the handful of people inside the bar. He walked back to me and helped me up. "Max, I'm really sorry about all that, drinks on the house tonight, however many you want. You okay?" He patted my shoulder.

A combination of tears and blood obscured my eyes.

"They got you pretty good. Don't worry, though, I can help clean you up no problem," Ryoz said, but I ran away, out the backdoor of the pub, straight to Mr. Cole's house.

I threw together a bag of clothes and some food and sprinted outside. It was strange to be the only one in such a hurry while everyone around me was having a relaxing evening of drinks, dinner, dessert, and entertainment. Necromancers performed musical numbers with skeletons on the street corners. Laughter, cheers, and applause could be heard on every block.

Everyone seemed so cheery. *Why can't that be me?*

As I headed north to the city gate, I stopped off in front of a stone, two-story building on Venom avenue. I knocked several times before there was an answer.

"Hello?" Someone I didn't recognize opened the door.

"Yeah, hi, I'm, uh…" I had a mental slip. *Who did I even come to see?*

"Are you okay? You look like you got attacked pretty bad."

"Yeah. Is Megan home?" I finally remembered the name.

The woman at the door frowned. "I'm sorry, she's gone for the weekend making some deliveries. I can leave her a note if you'd like?"

I feigned a smile. My lips quaked. I wanted to say something but I couldn't, so I left from the doorstep. I pulled out the slip Telyos gave me from my pocket, but the therapist office was closed. Without a second thought, I ran until I was entirely out of the Nezura gates.

12

I hiked for days until I made it to southwestern Lavarund, arriving at the National Park.

Ryoz was right: there was much isolation, but it wasn't the medicine I thought I needed. I could still hear the laughter from my classmates years later in the back of my mind, clearer than ever. Trudging through the forests, I eventually found myself in a valley, and something caught my eye. A shovel was on the ground, in the middle of two hills, glistening from the moonlight. It was late, and I thought I'd be more tired, but I had a spark of energy and an idea. I picked it up and started digging a hole.

I couldn't believe my eyes. After constantly shoveling for what felt like days, but only hours, I discovered the bones of a dinosaur, and with closer analysis, a velociraptor. My mind exploded with cheers like a fireworks celebration.

This would be it; this would be my revenge I would exact on all those that ran me out of town, bullied me, or tried to kill me.

I uttered the incantation, unsheathing the blade my uncle gave me many years ago. I stabbed my hand at what I thought was the precise moment, but there was a pinch. Still, my hand glowed. Holding my freshly cut palm over the pile of bones, my blood spilled. Any moment the remains would glimmer and assemble before my very eyes.

Any moment.

Okay, but seriously, any moment now.

Now?

"Vlark it all!" I spiked the shovel against the wall of soil and threw my hands on my head as I tried to rip out all of my hairs. The tears I cried from all the trials I had experienced now changed into the tears of a failed necromancer. It was all I knew how to do, it was all I ever loved, and it was all I wanted to improve at. I tried to echo the advice from Telyos in my head and believe it, but it couldn't remedy the depression. It seemed like every necromancer under the moon was better than me. All the beginners appeared to be way ahead. They mastered the focus and meditations. They knew how to say the incantations with perfect rhythm. They knew how deep to make cuts against the skin without pain, and they could perform spells without even referencing a book.

"Who am I kidding?" I moaned as I slumped against the wall and sat down. I was drowning in a flood of misery.

Maybe my parents and bullies from Verrenna were right, and I'm just bad at everything.

The moon was full and massive. I gazed up at it, hoping for some burst of inspiration. Suddenly, a person's head hovered over the hole I was digging—I couldn't see their face, but they were staring at me, the whites of their eyes exposed.

"You found something impressive," the old voice said.

"Who are you? What do you want?" I demanded with a broken up, syrupy voice.

"I can sense the power emanating from those bones. You've done well to discover them, Maximilian. That's a powerful friend at your feet."

"Who are you? How do you know my name?"

"Having trouble conjuring the summoning spell, are you?"

"Dammit, just tell me who you are!"

The old voice sighed. "I'm Akara."

I gasped. "Good joke, now please, tell me who you are!"

She disappeared from the top and reappeared next to me with a sudden *whoosh*. I could see her now, her short white hair glimmering from the moonlight.

"You have much to learn, young Maximilian, and I will be your personal mentor."

"What are you talking about? This must be a mirage. Everyone in Nezura said you died years ago in the attack against King Mozer."

"People can speculate and spit out their uninformed rumors, but I've always been around. I've seen the future of this country, and you are desperately needed for what is about to happen. It starts with me training you, helping you carve a path."

I peered at her, not knowing how to respond. It must have been a dream.

She held out her palms and uttered the incantation, stabbing her hand as the tip of her blade glowed white. The movements were fluid and confident. Her wrists glowed, and so did the bones. They magically assembled together, more lively than they had been for millions of years. Standing before us was the skeleton of a velociraptor, looking at Akara as her true master, waiting for her next command.

"Still don't believe that I'm Akara?" she said.

I shook my head.

As I held up my hand to the skeletal velociraptor, it studied me. It nudged its head against my palm like an affectionate dog.

"Already, you show promise for great talent. Skeletal conjurings take a liking to you; you embody a respectful aura. You don't see these summons as a tool, but more than that. By that metric alone, you're way ahead of the curve," Akara said.

"You're lying. Don't you know? I'm a joke among my peers!" My voice cracked as the tears still leaked from the corners of my eyes.

"Come here for a moment. I want to hug you; I can tell it's been a while," Akara stated.

I sniffled and quivered before stepping to the other side of the hole. When I was within arm's reach of her, she slapped my face.

"Ow!" I shrieked, my face stinging.

"Sorry, I don't have any cold water to throw in your face. You needed some sense to return to you. Now please, give me a hug because I do believe you need one."

I rubbed my cheek, scowling at her, but she opened her arms. After stepping closer once again, she wrapped me in a warm hug that rejuvenated my spirit. Even if it was a placebo or magic, my anguish alleviated.

"Let's diagnose all of your problems." Akara put her hand over my face, and her palm glowed as my head felt like it was dipped in a warm vat of honey. She pulled her hand away and looked at me with sympathetic eyes. Just as she was about to speak, she sighed. "I really want to yell at you, but that's not going to do you any good. Can you truly not see why other necromancers your age appear to be so much better than you?"

I shook my head.

"It's because you never mastered the small and basic skills. You did them, yes, but you didn't master them. When it got too hard, you gave up. It's time we go back to the beginnings."

"But I passed my classes when I took them at Nez—"

"You passed them because of your age and the folly of the instructors. As annoying as it may sound, you need to focus on summoning flowers and then work your way up to the skeleton of a chipmunk, a squirrel, or a rabbit even. We need to start from the ground up. Master those skills so that summoning the skeleton of a small dog will be no harder than boiling a pot of soup."

I hung my head. "I don't even know how to make soup."

Akara stared at me with slight irritation. "It appears you have more to learn than I had imagined." She smiled, then stared back at the velociraptor. It stood perfectly still, like a knight awaiting orders.

"Give her a name," Akara said to me, looking at her own work with hardly as much admiration as I did.

"You want me to name the velociraptor for you?"

"Sure, but she'll be your companion. I'll release control to you, and she'll follow your every command. Just give her a name."

"Uh, I'll call her, um, Betty? I always quite liked that name." I shrugged.

"Very well, Betty." She faced the dinosaur, whispering an incantation with my name sprinkled in.

The velociraptor looked at me as if awaiting the next command.

"Wow, I don't know what to say. Thank you so much!" I said, beaming at Akara.

"I'm going to head out now. You're going to come to my island home. I already have another guest staying with me who is undergoing training. You must come if you have any interest in getting better and saving the country. Do you understand?"

"Saving the country?" I echoed, remembering she mentioned it just a moment ago, but it hit me with tremendous confusion. I couldn't process it. "Are you sure you have the right person?"

"Quite sure."

"Maybe there's a different Maxi—"

"No. And there's no time to keep debating this. It's you, and you need to come to my home. See you there." She stared up at the opening.

I nodded. "But wait! Are you leaving? Why can't we go together?"

"Trust me, I've seen this outcome. If I go with you, we actually have less chance of survival."

"Less chance of survival?" I croaked.

"That's right. Please don't be afraid, just come to my island, and everything will be fine." She stepped up to me and pressed her thumb against my forehead. It radiated for a second, and the internal map of my surroundings became more familiar. "There, now you know the way to get to my island home. A skeletal oarsman will take you to my island. You'll meet him on the northern port of Lostonia." She gazed up at the top of the hole, closing her eyes and bending her knees slightly.

"Wait! Is there anything else I should know? You're just dumping this whole journey on me."

"Oh yes. There's a 50% chance you'll become best friends with the other person that's training on my island. If you do, the country has a significantly better chance at surviving. So please be kind to them but don't overdo it. Find a good balance."

"The country has a better chance at surviving what? You need to tell me!" I yelled irritably. "You can't possibly expect me to save it from anything! I'm just a loser!"

Akara smiled. "We'll work on your attitude. It's been good to meet you. See you on my island soon," she said, whooshing out of the hole and out of sight completely.

Betty tilted her head at me, and I stared back at her with goggle-eyed wonder.

"I guess we better get a move on, Betty."

Standing at the bottom of the hole, I didn't quite plan out how I would get out. I tried digging my fingers in the wall of soil, but I wasn't strong enough to keep climbing. Every attempt ended with layers of dirt falling like grains of sand in an hourglass as I sank. Betty watched, and eventually, she nudged me when I slid back down.

"What? Can't you see I'm already struggling enough?"

She lowered her entire body closer to the ground as if to say, "Hop on."

"I hope you know what you're doing," I uttered as I swung my right leg over her back, mounting her like a horse.

Betty sprang in the air using the power of her hind legs, clawing her way up the hole with relative ease. We reached the top in a blink of an eye.

"Yahoo!" I chuckled victoriously. "Why didn't you say something sooner!" I patted her smooth ivory neck. She turned halfway around, acknowledging my comment with a nod.

We stood there for a moment. I was trying to adjust myself to the world with my newly expanded mental map. I knew we were in Lavarund's National Park, located in the southwest portion of Lavarund, complete with massive forests and rolling hills. I needed to head directly north to get to Lostonia's port and travel across the Bolt Sea.

"Let's go, Betty." I leaned forward, and she galloped ahead.

The bright stars acted as our compass, guiding us north. Paired with a full moon, the night hardly felt dark. It wasn't long before we found a dirt path, which was the park's main trail. I thought it would be better if we ran alongside it, rather than on it, in case we ran into any travelers. It was late summer, and the weather was already starting to cool off, making it a popular time for visitors to camp out.

We were cruising along, gentle breezes reinvigorating my spirit, but my heart sunk as soon as I heard some voices coming from the trail. I tightened my legs around Betty's torso, and she came to an immediate halt. She lowered herself as if she knew we had to keep quiet and out of sight. Fortunately, the grass was high enough to keep us covered.

"And I really can't say it enough, but I'm so happy to be here right now, away from everyone," a man said.

"Yeah? Anything else going on you want to talk about?" another man replied.

I poked my head just above the grass, peered through the trees, and saw two men atop horses, carrying lanterns at their sides. They were strolling at a snail's pace.

"It would be nice to get this off my chest." The man sighed. "My daughter has—now please, you must keep this between you and me. No utterance of this to anyone, understand?"

"Of course."

"My daughter has been teaching herself necromancy."

"You can't be serious?"

"I wish I wasn't. I caught her in her bedroom, summoning the skeleton of a-a…" The man shivered. "…a dead mouse."

"That's disgusting!"

"I know, I know. I have no idea what I'm going to do."

"They have special cities with programs now where you can send her for that sort of thing, and they'll take care of her. I've heard nothing but good from 'em."

"Yeah, I know. I just want to see if maybe I can correct it myself. I don't want to give up my little girl to strangers."

"If it's too stressful at home, though, it might be best to send her away. She'll thank you in the long run. Better than having the Silver Army knock down your door. They take it so seriously."

"I just want her to stay far away from the Southeast."

"What's there?"

"Are you serious? Neh-Neh-Nezura." He shuddered. "Even if she went to Orbavue, that would be horrid."

"Calm down, she's not going over there. She's a good girl from what I've seen. Nezura is a town of filthy rejects. Besides, I think King Mozer is going to take care of them soon."

"What makes you say that?"

"I mean, you know the king's stance on those pesky 'mancers. He wants their whole society to collapse. He did away with their savior, Akara, and now they're really crumbling. I wouldn't be surprised if he sent the Silver Army down there to finish 'em off."

"Gosh, you certainly know a lot about this. But that would really be something, wouldn't it?"

"Yeah, so tired of having to share Lavarund with them. Have you ever met a 'mancer?"

"Aside from my wannabe daughter, no, I haven't. Thank goodness. They're putrid souls. I've got no interest in interacting with them."

"I've never met one either, but I had a few friends who bumped into one on the road one night; they almost took care of him themselves, but he got away. A damn shame."

"Hey, how come the horses have stopped?"

The horses stared directly at Betty, even though she was entirely covered by the grass. My heart sputtered in my chest. I could see the men's faces peering in our direction through the glow of their orange lanterns.

"This is odd," one of the men remarked.

"I wonder if the horses see something in the trees?"

"Obviously, they do; otherwise we wouldn't have stopped. Use your brain now."

"I don't like this."

I really ought to go up to them right now, command Betty to tear them apart limb from limb with her vicious jaws. Make them wish they had never said such foul, uninformed opinions. I could do it. They're right there. No one would ever know; no one else is around. The power in Betty's claws could make them beg. All I had to do was just say the word. Perfect opportunity to exact my revenge; yes, I could start with them.

"Come on, let's keep moving." The men pulled the reins on their horses, and they continued their slow trot on the path. I waited until they were far enough away before I patted Betty on the neck, and she raised her head. I gave one last look in their direction and sighed. "Let's not waste any time," I uttered.

Betty sprinted ahead while I rode on her back, dodging trees as we continued our trek north.

14

King Mozer found himself walking down a corridor in the castle with a tall, broad-shouldered man by his side. His face had chiseled features, but he recognized the angles.

"Father, you're not supposed to be here," King Mozer said.

"Is that how you greet your deceased parent?"

They drifted together on a straightened path, but Mozer couldn't turn left or right; he was anchored forward. His feet stepped ahead without his control.

"What's the meaning of this!" Mozer peered down the hall, which continued to stretch on for an eternity.

"Do you remember the day when we had that talk? About how no one would respect you because you'll only be known as my son? Until you're old, and I mean *old*, the people of Lavarund will only see you as a prince. An immature, cocky prince who was given royalty only for being born to the right family."

"I remember."

His father grinned the same devilish way as his son. "And I groomed you to be who you are today. Far more heartless than your mother or me, you were going to stun the world. My life was sheltered, and it came as a surprise to be disrespected when I took the throne. I made damn sure that would not happen to you. And you know what you did?" He paused as he waited for Mozer to answer, but Mozer knew how to manipulate the chess-match conversation with his father.

"I became far more successful than you could have ever dreamed. People don't remember your legacy, but more importantly, the people of Lavarund fear me," Mozer stated.

His father held a tight-lipped grin. "I showed you this. You remember this day?"

A door suddenly appeared in front of them, and they halted. King Mozer kicked it open without hesitation, glaring at his father.

"Tsk tsk," his father said, "your antics will only hold you back."

"Go ahead, lead the way, show me again for the millionth time!"

They stepped through the doorway, entering a chamber in the basement of the castle. His father teleported deeper inside, down an aisle of cellars. Mozer kept his head forward while groans of pain came from his periphery. Going through another iron door, they entered a prison of stone walls. A man was chained up against the center, cuffs around his ankles and wrists. His father approached the man with a sword, looked back at his son, and scowled. "Why are your eyes closed?"

King Mozer smirked. "Because I've seen this a million times in my dreams. My childhood was scarred by this event."

"You mean blessed by this event!"

"Sure. But I'm not going to give you the satisfaction this time." Mozer kept his eyes sealed when he heard the blade glide out from the sheath and swipe through. When he opened his eyes, he saw himself as a 10-year-old boy, staring ahead, jaw ajar.

"You should give me your respect."

"Why? Just because you're my father?" Mozer mocked.

"Let me show you something," his father said, and the walls around them faded into a different room.

Mozer found himself in the giant confines of a familiar house. Blood stained Mozer's armored plate that Leopold Smith had designed for him. Leopold was on the ground, motionless, covered with stab wounds, and Mozer clutched the bloodied sword.

"I was proud of you that day." His father stepped by his side and put his hand on Mozer's shoulder. "But you did something which also made me so disappointed."

Mozer grinned.

"You can lap it up all you want, but it might come back to haunt you, like I can in your sleep."

"You're hardly a haunting." Mozer snickered.

His father pointed ahead to a preteen boy escaping from the house.

"You let him go."

"He was just a kid, for cryin' out loud."

"And you didn't stop him," his father scolded.

"And you want to know why? Because I think it's eviler that I torture him with that memory. Besides, this happened years ago. Why do you even care?"

"You didn't stop him."

"You said that already!"

"You didn't stop him."

"I'm about to vlarking stab you myself! Why does it matter?"

His father's voice shifted to a female voice he recognized. "Because I'm going to stop you."

Mozer's blood ran cold. He stammered backward and locked gazes with Akara. She stepped closer to him.

"I already killed you," Mozer said, hiccupping with anxious laughter.

Akara marched forward with fire blazing in her pupils. Mozer stopped himself from stepping further backward. "I've already killed you." He grinned. "Since none of this is real, you know what? I'm actually glad you're here because you want to know what I've been dreaming about ever since that day I stopped you? Come now, why don't you give me another kiss?" He leaned his head forward and closed his eyes, but searing pain erupted through every bone of his body, forcing him to scream.

Mozer shot up in his bed, covered in sweat, shivering. He was overcome with nausea for a moment. The woman lying next to him in bed sat up and stared at him with her head tilted. "Is everything all right?"

"Don't ask questions! Just go back to vlarking sleep!" Mozer jumped off the bed and ran to the bathroom connected to his master bedroom. He sat in there until he felt his body and mind reach a state of homeostasis before climbing back into bed. For the rest of the night, he couldn't fall asleep.

It wasn't until Betty and I cleared the trees and reached open farmland and valleys when my nerves caused me to tremble. Fortunately, it was around 1 AM, and we still had a few hours before the early risers tended to their livestock and chores.

As we neared 2 AM, we made it atop a hill. I could see the dark, blocky buildings of Lostonia on the horizon and the wooden port with docks stretching out like fingers on the water. It was strange how I knew I had to go to the dock furthest to the left. To do that, Betty and I still had to sneak through the town, but it was asleep for the most part, except for the Silver Army knights required to patrol the streets all evening.

When I looked over to the right side off in the distance, I saw the house Uncle Leopold used to own. It was nothing more than a block of shadow in the night, and still, it was too much to handle. Thoughts of walking by crossed my mind, but I knew it would haunt me.

Did they even give him a grave in the Lostonia cemetery?

Just as my eyes brimmed with tears, I focused back on the task at hand.

I prayed Betty and I would come away unseen, but it was a risky stealth mission Betty and I were about to undertake. The large, rectangular two-story houses would provide us adequate shelter as we darted in between the smoothed-over stone streets. It was a famous port town with many exclusive jobs that paid relatively well. Even without Betty, I stuck out like a sore thumb with my poor man's rags.

I rubbed the side of her neck when I felt mentally prepared, and she sprinted ahead. Entering the city, we ran underneath the canopies where they had their open-air markets that welcomed travelers. We snuck down an alley as soon as the Silver Army guards meandered in our direction. Against the wall, Betty ducked down and became a statue as I held my breath.

Turning my neck around, I faced the street from the alley. I could see two guards stopping right at the end. Fortunately, there was a canopy and a large oak table giving us some cover. The twinkle from their silver-plated armor caught my attention, and I could see the red Lavarund flag painted around the arm.

"I love the Silver Army and King Mozer, but I can't help but feel bored out of my wits in this town night after night," one of the guards said with a sigh.

"Just be thankful you're stationed in Lostonia. This is a destination post. I'm sure people over in Orbavue would love to trade places with you," the other replied.

"I'd just like some action for once. The highlight of the last two years was being called back to the castle and defending it from that wench Akara."

"Why can't you just enjoy where you're at? This town's at peace. You've won the Silver Army lottery. Just drink some mead on the job like me, makes it go quick." The guard chuckled.

"Preposterous! What if we had an intruder? Must have a sober mind."

"Easy there, youngin'; booze gives me some confidence. And I don't get drunk, just a nice buzz. It's hardly a crime."

My stomach curdled into a hardened pit, and my adrenaline flowed as I imagined sicking Betty on both of them. While she feasted, I'd whip up a bone-crushing curse, only castable by experts, which I couldn't dare to do, but in my rage-fueled daydream, I could. *Yet, would that really do anything for me?*

Betty nudged my shoulder.

"What is it?" I whispered, turning around, and then my heart sank.

There was an amber glow coming from the window next to us. Betty tiptoed closer to it.

"Are you crazy!" I scolded in a whisper. "Stop right now! I command you to cease! Halt! Dammit, Betty!" I peeked through the window. A translucent curtain obscured our view, enough for us to be unseen.

There was a girl at a desk, no more than ten years old. She sat next to the soft glow of her lantern with the bones of a small animal sprawled in front of her. She was uttering something as she brought up a knife from underneath the desk. The blade's tip glowed a blinding white. As she pierced her hand, blood spilled on the remains. She smiled as the bones transformed from dirt-stained to bleach white. They assembled together magnetically, forming a ferret, which she hugged as soon as it tilted its curious head at her.

A thump hit the wall, and the girl panicked. She blew out the light in the lantern, and then I could hear the faint sounds of her scrambling to bed.

I was shaken to my core. Her disappointment was infectious.

Oh, how I wanted to break in and rescue that girl and bring her to where she'd have a promising future in Nezura, and then she'd—

Betty turned her neck to me, hanging her head. Her look conveyed the message, "We should get going."

I leaned forward, and Betty tiptoed down the alley, making our way to the left of the city. Slipping down the paths, we didn't have any more close calls. A few Silver Army guards patrolled further away on the other side of Lostonia, but we weren't near any of them. I was riding high on good fortune. Just as we reached the end of town, we had a clean break at the docks, but Betty rooted herself to the ground as we stood behind a two-story house.

"Come on, come on!" I whispered.

Betty wrapped her tail around my mouth.

Betty! Is this some kind of joke or prank? How come—

"I swear, I thought I heard some conspicuous tapping," said a Silver Army guard from the other side of the main street.

"Let's do an alley sweep," another guard suggested.

I gulped as sweat formed on my brow.

"What's the point? I don't want my shift going over. You're always so paranoid, Reginald," the other guard complained.

"Well, I suppose I'll start on one since—"

"Go ahead and waste your time. C'mon, when's the last time we've had any trouble?"

The other guard incoherently grumbled, and their armor plates clinked together as they walked away.

Betty unraveled her tail around my mouth.

"Phew," I whispered. "I'm so sorry if I doubted you earlier." I chuckled like a madman that just had his life saved. "Betty knows best, that's for sure!"

Betty made a go for it, with me still riding on her bony back, and we arrived at the wooden docks. We headed left and stopped at the edge, gazing out into the smooth, black, and glassy lake stretching to infinity. The star-littered sky reflected onto the expansive aquatic mirror. To my left, I saw a white cylinder float up through the water like a hot knife through butter, hardly making a splash.

A skeleton wearing a large, round hat made of sturdy ivory looked at me. "Hello. You must be Maximilian. Get in," he said, unenthused and disinterested.

"That's correct, uh, how were you summoned? How did you know I would arrive?" I asked.

"Do you really care?" he said with a bored tone.

I flinched, surprised by his response. "Yes, I do. I'm trying to understand how to become a better necromancer."

"Yeah, but do you really care that much for me to bore you with all the minor details? Which, in turn, would force me to talk to you further?"

"Sorry, I didn't mean to twist your arm, just curious about—"

"Will you just get in this boat already?" he asked.

"But I don't even know your name."

"Get. In," he stated.

"Okay, sorry, but how will I get my—"

Betty bunny-hopped into the boat, landing without a sound. I was still saddled on Betty's back, taking a moment to collect my thoughts. Sliding off her, I sat down cross-legged in the ivory boat while Betty curled up like a dog.

"Thank you." The skeleton sighed as the boat glided along the water and cut through the calm sea. "The name's Carl, if you absolutely have an undying curiosity to know."

"Nice to meet you, Carl. I'm Maxi—"

"Yes, we've already established who you are."

I wanted to inquire further about the magic used to summon him, but I didn't want to deal with his snarky attitude. I hadn't interacted with too many freestanding skeletons, but the ones I had met were much friendlier.

As our boat skated across the sea, only the stars and the moon lit up our path, until I noticed something twinkling on the left of the horizon.

"Carl, I hate to be a bother, but what's happening over there?" I said.

"Don't know, don't care." He stared ahead.

"It almost looks like a ship?" I squinted and leaned my head forward.

Carl sighed. "We can get a closer look." The boat took a diagonal turn.

As we came closer, Carl jerked the boat forward. "This is as far as I'll take you."

"It's probably best that way." My jaw dropped as my blood ran cold. "That's a Silver Navy ship!"

"Great. Keep your voice down."

"I wonder why it's not moving?"

"Ya ever hear the expression curiosity killed the cat? Geez-Louise, you ask a lot of questions." Carl groaned.

Betty shot her head up as if she heard an explosion, but it was utterly silent on the waters. She stared at the massive silver ship and then scrambled to the tiny boat's opposite side, trembling.

"What's the matter?" I started petting Betty on the side of her body. Looking back towards the ship in the distance, I saw the crew hauling something up from the water. It was a giant net carrying a massive pile of sharp white objects. "What could that be?"

"I think it's a bunch of skeletal remains," Carl noted.

"How come Betty's so afraid? Do you sense anything coming from there?" I asked.

"I don't know, but I don't like it, that's for sure," Carl said.

"Should we move closer over there?"

"Don't be ridiculous, I shouldn't have changed the path in the first place. We're heading straight towards Akara's house now, and that's final."

"Sorry, Carl."

He didn't reply, but we did steer back to our original route. I tried to relax Betty, but she wouldn't stop shaking. Even wrapping my arms around her and petting her head couldn't alleviate her stress.

The sun was poking out from the horizon, haze appeared over the water out of nowhere, and I couldn't see anything in front of me for a few seconds. Then the fog disappeared in the blink of an eye, and we were in front of a tiny island I didn't see earlier. The island had a few palm trees on the edges and a rounded stone house with circular windows in the center—a friendly, inviting home.

The boat came up to the shore and stopped abruptly. Betty ceased quivering, and the two of us stepped in the shallow water of the beach.

"Thank you, Carl."

Carl nodded and kept glancing at me and back at the water. "Look, I'm really sorry about being rude to you earlier. Forgive me. It's just in my curmudgeon nature."

"I understand, I guess." I shrugged.

"And you've learned a valuable lesson, not all skeletons are summoned the same." Akara stepped forward.

I didn't even hear her approach.

"Hello, Akara." Carl waved.

"Thank you for bringing my guest. You're relieved of your post; have a good day," Akara said.

"Thank you." Carl bowed and sank into the water, out of sight.

"I'm glad you made it." Akara pulled me in for a hug, a warmth that reminded me of Uncle Leopold.

"I can't believe I'm here in front of you; it feels like a dream. *The* Akara has asked me to be here!" I cracked up. "I'm in her secret island home! This is insane!"

She smiled at me.

"I was a loser, well, still am, but you asked—"

"Okay, okay, that's enough. Don't view yourself like that, and I'm not going to coddle you. No negative attitudes or this won't end well, believe me." Akara glared.

"Understand." I straightened my posture as if she were an admiral.

Akara took notice of Betty and walked over to cradle her head.

"What happened to her? Why is she upset?" Akara said.

"Oh, uh, yeah, it was the strangest thing. We were gliding through the water on our boat when we passed a Silver Navy ship lugging a massive pile of bones."

Akara's eyes widened. "Was it a large pile of little bones or gigantic bones?"

"Gigantic bones, I believe. But we were kinda far away, so it was tough to say for sure."

"The Zevolra." Akara—the necromancer's fiercest warrior and leader that had ever existed—had the look of genuine horror on her face. "They found it already."

"Sorry, but can we start from square one with the Zevolra-thing?" I asked. "I mean, they talked about it in school briefly, but it was glazed over since I came in late and it was taught to younger kids. So, whenever it was brought up, I never really got it," I said. I was afraid Akara would scold me, but all I heard was silence. I couldn't look her in the eye.

Akara took a moment to answer. "The Zevolra is an ancient monster, its existence was speculated, but I always knew it was true. I could feel it deep in the Earth. The most powerful summon that could ever be made by a necromancer."

"Whoa. I believe it too. The bones they hauled up were ginormous. Do you have a picture of it in a textbook or something?"

"Come inside the house, I have a painting I can show you, and you can also meet Wynn." Akara strode towards the house, and I jogged behind her, Betty following.

"Gee, I have so many questions for you, like, I thought you died, yet here you are, and then I start thinking about it more, and I freak out, like, what if I just died?"

Akara spun around, irritated. "Everything will be explained to you. No, you did not die. This isn't a mirage." She paused and peered into my eyes. "Now, let's take a tour of where you'll be staying."

She led me through the front door of the small stone house, entering a living room with dark red cushioned chairs and a fireplace with a relaxing flame. Betty stopped in front of it and curled up in a ball.

"She's already making herself at home." Akara chuckled, guiding me further into the house.

The entire home had a tan hardwood floor, which made it feel like a cozy cottage. To my right was a dining room, which connected directly to a kitchen, where the aroma of bacon, eggs, and pancakes wandered through the air, thanks to a skeletal chef.

"How did you know to make my favorite food?" I beamed.

Akara turned to me. "I could sense your thoughts earlier when we met. Don't worry, I wasn't invasive. I just wanted to make you feel right at home."

We walked down a tiny hallway with three different bedrooms. She took me to the bedroom all the way to the left and opened the door.

"This is where you will be staying," Akara said.

I poked my head in. There was a small bed with a desk underneath a window letting in the sunshine.

"Looks cozy." I smiled.

"There's a closet in there too with clothes that should fit you."

"I have so many questions, but maybe you'll answer them later." I eyed her suspiciously, wondering how she knew my clothing sizes.

Akara turned back around and knocked on the door in the middle of the hallway.

"Wynn? Can I open the door?"

"It's your house," an annoyed voice replied.

"Yes, well, you are my guest, and I don't want to intrude." Akara turned the knob and pushed open the door.

Wynn sat at her desk by the window; the room looked identical to mine. Her back was toward us. All I could see was her long black hair, which had a jagged red streak that ran from top to bottom like a lightning bolt. With a closer look, I noticed she was tossing flames back and forth between her hands. The flames evaporated in a microsecond. She turned around, glanced at me, then back at Akara.

"Whatcha need?" she asked.

"I'd like for you to come out to the dining room. I want to introduce you to our guest while we have breakfast."

"Kay." She took a deep breath and stood up, taller than both of us, wearing loose white pajamas.

The three of us wandered into the dining room, and the tables were set with plates of food stacked high enough for the three of us.

When I sat at the table, I looked up and saw a painting of a stormy night over a sea, where a bright orange, four-legged monster was flying in the air with gigantic claws. Seven horns jutted from its crown, its mouth was wide open, showcasing its wicked fangs, and it had ten blue eyes that formed a circle on its head.

I shuddered. "That's painted in the ceiling of the Nezura Municipality Building. That's the Zevolra, right?" I pointed.

"Yes, and those are the remains I believe the Silver Navy has captured." Akara sighed, piling her plate with eggs, bacon, and pancakes.

"You've got to be vlarking me." Wynn dropped her fork.

"By the way, Maximilian, this is Wynn," Akara said.

"Uh, hi, pleasure to meet you." I stuck out my hand.

"Hi." She gave it a shake, her hand felt limp, and she pulled it back like a frog's tongue capturing a fly.

"Wynn, here, is a once-in-a-generation talent. She's a Vyrux."

I dropped my jaw and did a triple take at her. "I'm sharing a home with a Vyrux and the most revered necromancer that has ever lived?!"

"And what's so special about you?" Wynn said, fixing her attention on her food as she ate with proper manners.

"Now now, let's not get into a stone measuring contest here. Both of you still need to learn about your abilities, which is why you are here. King Mozer is planning on launching an all-out war on Nezura. He plans on killing every last one of the necromancers and would love nothing more than to kill Wynn."

"Does he even know she exists? I didn't even know that a Vyrux existed. Isn't that the thing in the history books? Usually mentioned with the Zevolra? She must be ancient."

"I'm twenty-one," Wynn snapped.

Akara stifled laughter but straightened up and said, "They appear every thousand years to a family of necromancers and—"

Wynn cleared her throat and glowered at Akara.

"Sorry, I didn't mean to make you uncomfortable," Akara said.

I stared at Wynn as if she were an animal in a zoo.

"Why don't you paint a portrait? It'll last longer." Wynn fixed her attention to her food.

"I'm sorry, I don't mean to stare." I shifted my gaze down to the table.

"To answer your question from earlier, Mozer is unaware of Wynn's existence. She has been kept secret and has lived most of her life on this island," Akara said.

"And it's driving me vlarking mad!" Wynn screamed.

"Watch your language." Akara's tone reminded me of a mother's.

"Imagine!" Wynn glared at me, pointing her butterknife and jabbing it forward. "Imagine having to spend all of your time in your teens cooped up in this house! I'm twenty-one, and I've still never kissed a boy! I've never gone out with my friends for my birthday to get vlark-faced drunk in Nezura! Everything has been ripped away from me, and for what? Because I can do this?" Wynn jumped from her seat and formed a fireball from her palm that hovered over the table, spinning rapidly. The heat seared my forehead as I fell backward in my chair.

"Wynn!" Akara scolded, and the fireball disappeared. Akara ran around the table, kneeling beside me. "Are you okay?"

17

"Yeah, I'm fine." I took a deep breath with my eyes wide open. "That was incredible."

Akara helped me back up and put my chair in place. A skeleton burst in from the kitchen.

"Hello, is everything all right?" the skeleton said in an innocent, worried voice. "My goodness, did my food do this to you?"

"No, Lawrence. Wynn just had a little outburst, that's all. The food has been terrific," Akara assured him. "Max, this is our chef, Lawrence."

"Hello, nice to meet you! And thank goodness, I was worried my food put him on his back. I'll be in the kitchen in case anyone needs anything." The skeletal chef stepped away.

"Sorry about that," Wynn said, going back to eating as if nothing had happened.

"That's okay, I understand your anger," I said.

"Do you?" Wynn gave me a side-eye.

I ignored Wynn and stabbed forkfuls of food.

"Now, Wynn, let's not get so upset with our guest. We have bigger things we need to worry about," Akara said.

"No, really, I understand," I blurted. "I mean, my struggles are a little different, but I feel like it's a similar pain. All the times I've tried to be a good necromancer and learn new abilities, I've always lagged behind. Constantly getting the worst grades, and I always felt like such an outcast. I was picked on by the other kids nonstop, not to mention before all of that, my parents were terrible." I sighed, burying my head in my palm. "Loneliness and failure have paid me too many visits."

Wynn kept chewing and didn't look up from her meal. "I'm sorry to hear that."

"It's okay. Akara caught me at a time where I was ready to give it all up. But in a turn of events I never saw coming, I'm now here with a girl that can spin flames, a legendary 'mancer, and a summoned velociraptor named Betty."

Betty, who was curled up by the fireplace, lifted her head and stood up. Wynn turned around, and her eyes widened as her lips curved up.

"A pet! We have a pet named Betty in the house now?" Wynn jumped out of her chair and wrapped her arms around Betty, petting the side of her body. "She's so cute! Is she really staying?"

"Yes, Betty will be staying with us. I think she'll do good to boost morale around here." Akara smiled at me.

"I think so too." I lowered my voice so only Akara could hear me. "Gosh, I just want to ask Wynn so many questions. So, she's a Vyrux? She can command flames at the will of her fingertips?"

"Not just flames, but she also possesses gale-force power. She will be able to do more with fire and wind with some training, but yes. Her fire and wind prowess are already admirable, but it's been a lot of hard work."

"I can only imagine."

"Get ready, because I will get started on you later. But first, we need to have a conversation about things. You thought I died, correct? And everyone else in Nezura and Lavarund believes I'm gone, yes?"

I nodded.

"I did die; that's actually true. Technically, I've died twice. This is my final life, and I'm spending it as wisely as I can."

I raised an eyebrow at Akara and leaned my head forward.

"Wynn already knows the story, but you don't, so allow me to explain.

"There's an ancient necromancer spell that allows you another life. In case you know you're going to die, or you're likely to die, you can keep on living if you pass away. There are some side effects, but as you'll learn, this was the only option.

"King Mozer, as you know, has spread hatred and vitriol against the necromancers. It wasn't always like that, but his parents, who were king and queen before him, sparked the oppression once they needed something to blame for the Southeast's drought. Since Nezura was already known as the necromancer hub and located in the Southeast, the king and queen blamed us for everything, which was never true. As you know, we're not able to curse land or weather.

"Anyways, Mozer was born, and once his parents died, he took the throne and continued the hatred of necromancers to an extreme. Tensions have been rising over the years, and currently, things are looking grim. You don't have to be a genius to know that he's trying to plot a course of action for a war he's almost guaranteed to win. And it irks me that King Mozer even goes around killing 'traitors' who do so little as to call him stupid. There's no freedom for necromancers or anyone.

"I thought my plan was solid. I started raising an army of skeletal warriors because I didn't want our people to die for the crusade. A necromancer's summons can be vicious, and that was all I needed. Then I learned one of the most potent necromancer spells that have ever existed: resurrection. You start by laying down in a place where you would like to be reborn once again, I chose this very house, and I stabbed myself with my own bone knife in the heart. It's a brutal spell, even for a master, and it requires much focus, the correct incantation, and being unafraid of stabbing yourself in the vlarking chest!

"A ghost of my body lay on the bed, and after I performed the spell, I was at 90% capacity and energy, and that's a side effect. You feel like you're not the same as you used to be. Almost like you're always in the mental and physical state of overcoming a cold. It was rough, but it had to be done, for I knew that my mission was a gamble.

"I stormed the castle with all of my skeletal warriors. Much blood was shed, and many from the Silver Army died in battle, although King Mozer will lie and say there were hardly any casualties. My skeletons did wonderfully. I broke inside the castle and entered the main chamber where I saw him, King Mozer.

"He was standing next to his assistant, who's a tall woman with plenty of muscles. A trained assassin that I was fully prepared for. Or so I thought I was.

'Go on, Lara, I don't need you here. I'll take care of her myself,' Mozer said. His voice had a hollowness with no room for compassion.

"Lara left the room, and just as I ran up to him to prepare for the bone-crushing curse, my body seized up. I didn't have enough energy. That missing 10% was what I needed to pull it off.

"And that's when I saw his smug smile. I was paralyzed. He crept towards me, and I'll never forget what he did next. He kissed me, the vlarking bastard kissed me, lips and tongue. Then I died, I died a sudden death that took less than a microsecond. I don't even know how it happened, but I experienced something unique when I died for the second time. All of the different futures that could occur flashed before my eyes. Which brings me to why you're here. Maximilian, you're needed, whether you believe it or not. You and Wynn are the only ones who can stop Mozer."

18

Lara stood outside the thick, black metal doors. When Lara was younger, she remembered the doors upstairs used to be wood, but now, wood was replaced with forged iron.

She banged on the entrance with the side of her fist, creating a low rumble. A simple knock wouldn't make enough sound. The two doors split open at the center, and Mozer slipped out, wearing nothing but a cloth over his groin. He was pale and lean and glanced up and down at Lara.

"The Silver Navy has found the remains you requested," Lara stated.

The glowing candlelight from the stone walls shined enough to illuminate Mozer's lips curling from ear-to-ear. "You mean, the remains of Zevolra? They've been found?"

Lara nodded. She could tell his mouth was watering.

"This is wonderful, wonderful news. Where is it?" Mozer leaned forward, his face just inches from Lara.

She took a deep breath. "It's at the Navy post east of Lostonia. They found it in the Bolt Sea."

"Take me to it right away, won't you?" Mozer asked.

"Right now?"

"Yes!" Mozer strode down the narrow purple carpet in the middle of the flagstone floor.

"Don't you want to tell whoever is in your bed where you're going?" Lara said with a hint of snark.

Mozer froze and turned around slower than molasses. He crept up to Lara, standing inches away from her. Lara didn't lean back or hesitate, even though her heart raced.

"I don't answer to anyone," Mozer said with a shaky voice, running his fingers through Lara's hair. However, she remained still, furrowing her brow. "It's just you and me here, darling." Mozer cupped the back of Lara's head and yanked her forward, locking her in for a kiss.

Lara shoved him away. "What are you doing?"

Mozer chuckled. "You're really the closest one to me; you of all people should know me better than anyone, yet it's taken me so long to do that."

"Why now?" Lara clenched her fist.

"I'm feeling on top of the world, darling. And you always held a certain fear over me, until now." Mozer winked.

"You really shouldn't force people to do things like that."

"You're right; normal people shouldn't, but I can." Mozer blew her a kiss.

"It's just you and me in this hallway. I could seriously hurt you; you know that, right?"

"Ah. Go ahead and try it then." Mozer leaned his head forward, flashing all of his teeth with a twisted grin.

"Put on some clothes and have some respect for the Silver Navy that worked endlessly to find your treasure," Lara snapped.

"Just for you," Mozer said, slipping back inside his room through the iron doors.

Lara prepared a double-suited carriage of thirty-six horses from the royal stables. She made sure the carriage was filled with Silver Army infantrymen and that all the door locks functioned. She also requested the kitchen staff to prepare a variety of meads for the short trip.

Mozer strolled down to the stables, carrying a cane with a crystallized skull at the top. The infantry waited in front of the carriage, saluting him as he moseyed by. Lara held the door open for him. "Onward and posthaste!" Mozer announced before settling into the velvet booth inside. Lara closed the door, and the stable gates rolled open, revealing the early morning fog. The cab driver hollered out, and the horses sprinted west.

Along their smooth journey, the fog lifted, and the sun filled the land with a pink-orange hue. Mozer had spotted a man and a woman riding horses yards away in a field. They were gawking at the royal carriage.

Mozer grinned. "Stop the cart!" he screamed.

"What? Why?" Lara asked.

"Don't talk back to me. I want this cart stopped now, so stop it!"

Lara glared back at Mozer and wrenched open the latch on the ceiling. A small ladder came down, followed by a gentle breeze. She hopped up the steps and trod on top of the double carriage to reach the front, where she told the driver to stop immediately. The cab driver swore and jerked the reins back, stopping all the well-trained horses without much delay. Lara went back down into the cabin.

"Get all the infantrymen out, now," Mozer stated as he hurried outside with his cane. He strolled towards the couple that had stopped and ogled.

Lara opened up the door to the Silver Army cabin and instructed all of them to stand by.

"Hello! Beautiful horses, I must say!" Mozer smiled at the man and woman who were trembling.

"Hi!" The woman beamed.

"Is it you? Is it really you?" The man glowed.

"Yes, it is. My oh my, your horses are beautiful, but this specimen in front of me, well, she's even more captivating." Mozer leered at the woman.

"Uh, you talkin' about the horse?" the woman asked.

Mozer chuckled and crept towards her. "Don't be daft."

"Uh-uh-that's my wife you're talking about." The man took a deep breath.

Mozer halted and spun towards the man with a wide-eyed glare. "Are you a traitor?"

"N-no s-sir -I mean- Y-Your Highness. I just wanted to let you know that she's w-with me in case there was any muh-misunderstanding."

Mozer grinned at the man on his horse for a moment. He twirled the cane in his hands back and forth before catching it and clubbing the horse's leg. It snapped like a twig. The horse screeched, falling over and crushing the man's thigh.

"AHHHH!" he wailed.

The woman gasped and slid off her horse.

"No! Marianne! Run away! Run away! Please!" the man screamed, pinned to the ground by the squealing horse.

Mozer smirked as he jumped towards the woman. Mozer lunged to grab her leg, but he missed as she hopped on her horse and trotted off in the distance at breakneck speed.

"You vlarking dolt!" Mozer bellowed, taking his cane and bashing it against the man's face. "I get whoever I want! Especially any man's wife! I'm the king, which means your property is mine!"

The man whimpered and cried as he dawned a crimson mask. Mozer cocked his head back and spit a massive glob on him. "Vlark off." Mozer sneered and stomped back over to his thirty-six horse-drawn carriage. He approached Lara and frowned. "I was in such a good, vlarking mood! Gimme all the mead in the cabin, now!"

The horses trotted along the countryside. Mozer glared out the window to his right, taking long pulls from the various meads held in the center of the cabin by a metal cupholder.

"Can't you go a little easy on the juice? It's barely morning, and I don't think you've eaten anything," Lara said.

"Why don't you worry about yourself?" Mozer gulped another mouthful of mead, scowling at Lara.

The rest of the ride was silent. Entering the Navy outpost's main gates, Mozer's lips curved up. The carriage crept inside the massive stables held together by evenly stacked gray stones. Inside, it reeked of hay and manure, but Mozer didn't care. He hopped out of the cabin first before the Silver Army could escort him. Mozer took off like a jaguar.

"Let's follow him to the storage house." Lara rolled her eyes and directed the Silver Army as they marched a few paces behind Mozer.

Mozer threw open the door that led to a hallway, and he skipped all the way down, taking a right and a left until he was in front of a massive arched iron entrance. Unable to contain himself, he shoved through the middle and marveled at the gigantic pile of bones surrounded by the Silver Navy. Several metal chandeliers were hanging from the ceiling, aglow with bright candles. A boulder-like skull sat front and center with a crown of spikes poking out. The rest of the bones were behind it in a disorganized mound.

Mozer's jaw dropped, and his limbs dangled like cooked noodles. He was entranced as he stepped closer, paying no attention to any of the crew even though they all froze in place to salute him.

"Admiral," Mozer uttered.

"What did he say?" a naval member whispered to the other.

"Who's the vlarking admiral of this post?!" Mozer screeched, echoing off the walls of the chamber.

A man wearing dark blue plated armor with jagged silver streaks across the chest stepped forward. "King Mozer." He saluted.

Mozer eyed the tall, muscular man. His pupils traced his mustache that matched his dark hair. "Very well done." Mozer slithered toward him. "What's your name?"

"You really don't remember me?"

"It's been a while, boy." Mozer's grin faded.

"Admiral Holtmeyer. We've met on a few occasions."

"Mhmm." Mozer's eyes narrowed. "All I wanted to say was, bravo."

"These are the remains you requested, yes?" Holtmeyer stood with a precise upright posture.

"Lemme take a gander." Mozer stepped away and circumnavigated the pile.

Lara and the rest of the Silver Army filed into the storage house. When Mozer came back around from studying the crevices and curves of bright ivory, he touched the tip of a rib that stuck out to the edge. Mozer shuddered. "You brilliant bastards! You found it!" Mozer sprinted back up to Holtmeyer and clutched his hand as he shook it emphatically. "You've done very well for the kingdom, and I do believe a promotion is in order." Mozer beamed.

"I'm honored. Thank you, but before we discuss anything further, I'm sorry, Your Highness, but what plans do you have for the remains? We've been searching for years, and we've finally acquired it. What now?"

Mozer's lips collapsed on both sides as he leaned his head forward. "My plans?" His eye twitched.

Holtmeyer winced for a microsecond, smelling the alcohol on the king's breath. "Perhaps I should rephrase. What would you like us to do next for you?"

Mozer's lips curled up. "I want you to kiss me."

Holtmeyer dropped his jaw and took a single step back. "I beg your pardon?"

Mozer lurched his head and locked his lips with Holtmeyer as he squirmed and tried to pry the king off him. All the Silver Military members gasped.

"What are you doing?" Holtmeyer finally shoved him away.

"I do whatever I want! And no questions shall be asked! Do you not trust your king to defend you from those dirty, blasphemous necromancers?"

Holtmeyer stepped backward as Mozer inched closer to him. Mozer held up his cane. The crystallized skull at the top twinkled from the chandelier light.

"We trust you! I just need to know what to tell my crew!" Holtmeyer said.

"Well then, if it's such a vlarking need, listen carefully. Every last one of you bleedin' vlarks listen, because I'm not gonna repeat myself!" Saliva scattered from Mozer's mouth. "These remains are highly sought after by those wretched 'mancers. This is a powerful tool that has more value than all your miserable lives put together. Once a week, I will come here to ensure that all you bloody idiots are doing your jobs by guarding this treasure. When I come in to inspect, you all must evacuate the room to give me utter privacy as I make sure nothing is touched. Is that understood?"

The room responded with silent nods.

"Good. Very good. Now get the vlark out of here and let me inspect every bone we have! It's gonna take me a while for inventory."

All the guards exited the storage house, and Mozer locked the door behind them.

Turning around, he approached the mountain of gigantic bones and smirked as he stood before the skull. He pulled off the crystallized head from the top of his cane, unsheathing an ivory knife. Staring wide-eyed at the blade, he whispered an incantation. With a stab of his hand, a blinding flash shot out and struck the head of the Zevolra.

✖ ✖ ✖

After breakfast finished up, Betty and I went outside to enjoy the breeze coming in off the Bolt Sea. We played fetch with a stick on the beach while waiting for Akara to join. Wynn was the first to leave the house, juggling a set of three fireballs with her hands, but her face looked disinterested while I stared in awe.

"All right, all right, let's start with you first today." Akara strode from the house and pointed at me.

"Uh, sure, what did you have in mind?" I said as Betty delivered the stick back to me.

"I need you to summon a simple bonefish." Akara dropped tiny white pieces on the sand. "You got your blade on you?"

I yanked it out from my pocket. "Right here!"

"Let's see what you got."

I took a deep breath, my heart rate kicked up, and I started overthinking the incantation. I needed to focus on a balance between bringing new life to the fish and uttering the magic words: *"Bones are vessels of the soul. I give my blood to bring life as toll. Rise within and become my companion. Awaken and r-rise, reform, and mend. Become one, once uh-again."*

The tip glowed. I crookedly pointed the blade at my hand all too fast, missing the palm's sweet spot.

"Ow!" I shrieked as I dug the glowing white blade in. The bones assembled together halfway, resembling a floating goldfish, but they collapsed into a lifeless scatter. I hung my head and sighed.

"It's okay, chin up, and give me your blade. Use mine. Let's try it again." Akara exchanged razors.

My breath stopped.

I'm holding Akara's legendary blade, which summoned an army of skeleton warriors, grizzly bears, lions, and other powerful magical creatures. It was a solid, dark purple handle, with a black line that rose through the ivory, like an intrusive tree root.

"Is it true you've summoned the remains of a unicorn with this blade?" I gaped.

"Yeah, it's a good blade. Give it a go; let's see what you've got."

"O-Okay, su-sure." I beamed at the remains and took a deep breath.

The incantation flowed through my mouth like a gentle river, no interruption, no stutter, no hiccup. The blade glowed white-hot, and I stabbed my hand with no hesitation. The pain was nonexistent, while blood rained on the ground.

Vlark yeah, that's how it's supposed to feel.

But the fish didn't resurrect.

How was that possible? That was probably the best incantation I've ever delivered. The concentration was there, the thoughts felt perfect, and there wasn't an ounce of pain. Why, why couldn't I—

The ground shifted beneath me.

Sand parted down the center of an object pulling itself from the ground. As it floated up, it became clear that I had summoned the bones of a full-grown great white shark. I stepped backward and tripped onto the ground. Betty backed away, and Akara smiled. I glanced back, and even Wynn was staring in awe. The shark bones glowed white, and it floated in the air as if it were inside an invisible tank.

"I don't believe it! I-I don't, ha!" I was on the verge of tears. "Akara, that's the largest summon I've ever conjured! This is so amazing! I did it! Me! This shark looks so beautiful and sturdy! You figured it out, Akara! It was my knife all along!"

Akara glared at me.

My internal joy fizzled out. "What's the matter?" I asked.

"My knife is cracked, dull, and old, not to mention, it's my backup knife. It's in horrible condition. Yours is actually far superior to mine, even better than my primary one! The problem was never the knife, but your inability to believe in yourself."

Even though Akara practically scolded me, I couldn't help but jump up and sprint over to Akara and wrap my arms around her in a tight bind.

"I'm not sure what this is for, but I didn't do anything," Akara said, returning a squeeze but the first to pull away from the hug.

"But you did. You believed in me when no one else really has." I beamed, on the verge of tears as I gazed at the floating bone shark. "Thank you, Akara."

"You're welcome, and while that was impressive and definitely makes things easier, there's still much to work on."

"Of course."

Betty ran up to me and nuzzled her head against my body as if to say, "I'm proud of you."

"By the way, who made you this knife?" Akara held it up to the sunlight, studying its curve, design, and craftsmanship.

"Why do you ask?"

"It's remarkable. Feels light as a feather, and it's extraordinarily sharp. How old is this thing?"

"Uh, my Uncle made it a long time ago. He made knives for necromancers. He himself was a necromancer in Lostonia but obviously kept it a secret."

"Well, the man certainly knew how to craft a knife. I'm jealous. This truly is one of the best knives I've seen. And I've had mine designed by a highly sought-after designer in Orbavue as a little girl." Akara returned my knife, and I gave hers back.

Wynn approached me and said, "You didn't give yourself enough credit earlier. Well done." Her smile disappeared like a blink. "I suppose my training comes next?"

"That's right, Wynn." Akara turned to me. "But Maximilian, please unsummon your shark. Even though I'm sure you want to stare at it all day, we will need the space."

"Sure thing," I said, excusing myself from the two of them as I yelled, *"Unsummon!"* to collapse the shark bones. "Do you mind if I listen to your lesson with Wynn?"

"Not at all." Akara turned and focused on Wynn. "I know your life hasn't been everything you wanted it to be, and I'm sincerely sorry about that. But the Vyrux has a duty on Earth, and it must be carried out."

Wynn crossed her arms. "You've told me all of this before."

"As much as you may not want to hear it, it's important to understand the significance. Every thousand years, evil tries to take over the world. They're usually kings or leaders, exactly like Mozer. The Vyrux is born to bring balance," Akara explained.

Hearing all this information was like being back in my Necromancer Legends class. I thought they were fables, just like everyone else, and I daydreamed through a lot of those lessons, but Akara's tone was dire. I had to listen.

"The Zevolra and the Vyro existed at the same time as galactic entities. The Zevolra contained rock and water as well as the Vyro fire and wind. They battled in space, and thus, Earth was created after the Vyro won the battle. The remains of the Zevolra fell, but when the Zevolra died, it gave life to Earth. We are technically all descendants of the Zevolra, but a core evil existed deep inside that was unleashed, and it terrorized the planet for thousands of years by tyrant leaders, unnoticed by the Vyro. Eventually, when the Vyro died, a core of justice took spiritual form and used human bodies as a vessel, bestowing a special power. This person is known as the Vyrux.

"The Vyrux exists once every thousand years, around the same time as the core evil from the Zevolra takes form. Fortunately, the Zevolra evil doesn't contain an elemental power, but they're usually brilliant minds. I firmly believe Mozer contains the Zevolra core evil. If Mozer kills Wynn, Lavarund will devolve into a state of disarray and chaos for a thousand years. And I've seen all the possible futures laid out in front of me, and they don't look good when Mozer steals the remains."

I shuddered. "Is it possible to get the remains from them? And then—stick with me here—we summon the Zevolra!"

Akara shook her head. "It would take a while to summon. But in the few outcomes where we discovered the remains first, we stormed the castle and overthrew Mozer."

"What happens in this reality, where Mozer beats us to the bones?"

Akara hung her head. "Unfortunately, that information was murky."

"Damn," I uttered. I suspected she knew but didn't want to disclose it.

"It's okay; we'll do what we can. Now, Wynn, you must learn to fly," Akara said.

"What do you mean by that? Like grow wings and take off?" Wynn arched her brow.

"No, I mean, you need to use your wind to propel from the ground with your heels. Right now, you can only shoot wind from the palm of your hands. We need to improve."

Wynn scoffed. "You think it's so easy, I don't even know how I would do that. The wind only channels from my arms to my fingertips."

"Yes, but every Vyrux that has ever existed has been noted as a flyer."

"Perhaps they meant this." Wynn opened her palms towards the ground and blasted herself upwards in a mighty spurt. She rocketed up fifty feet in the air, twirling before she dove into the sea.

"That was amazing!" I clapped and beamed.

Wynn emerged to the surface and grinned as she swam back to the shore.

"No, Wynn, they did not mean that." Akara shook her head. "In all the depictions, the Vyrux can sustain flight from her heels. It's documented that they can skate on the air using their wind power. It's not just a burst from the wrists." Akara picked up two stones on the sandy beach similar in size. "Let me show you an example." Akara tossed one with her right arm while the rest of her body remained still. Then she took the other rock and threw it much further as she put a step into it. "You see that, Wynn?"

"Big deal, I can throw rocks too." Wynn rolled her eyes.

"Yes, but did you see how much power I generated when I put a step into it? Your legs are a powerful tool, and you will need them to fly. The more tools you have on your side and the more refined they are, the better chance we have."

Wynn lost the angsty look in her eyes and nodded. "How do I channel the wind away from my wrists, then?"

"You didn't always know you could shoot wind from your palms, right? So, what you'll need to do is rediscover how the wind moves through your body. If it truly starts in your shoulders, how can you send it to your ankles? Try some meditation exercises, similar to the ones we were working on before Maximilian's arrival."

"How did the meditations help before?" I asked.

"Let me show you again." Wynn smirked as she held out her palm. Flames spun together out of thin air, creating a roaring fireball with blinding brightness and oppressive heat. It grew close to the size of the house as she held it over her head.

I fell back into the shallow water, gawking at the fire before it vanished.

"Then, a shot of that wind to propel the fire forward and BOOM!" Wynn cracked up. "Before the mediations, I could barely make a flame the size of a snowball."

As the weeks continued, I practiced more summoning with my own knife and fell into a groove, the likes of which I've never seen in myself. I was summoning so many small animals that I could do it in my sleep.

Betty was excellent company. She sat next to me and watched me magically reassemble the bones of chipmunks, rabbits, and squirrels. Each time I finished it successfully, she bounced up and down in celebration, making me giggle.

Akara focused most of her attention on Wynn as I sharpened my summoning. Wynn concentrated on meditation and channeling the wind energy from her arms to the bottom of her legs. Wynn seemed patient and quiet, but one day it ended in screaming.

"Wynn, a cool conscience always prevails," Akara said.

"That's so easy for you to say! You're not the one who has to pour all of their time and energy on one thing only to keep falling short. You were a natural necromancer talent. Spells came easy to you!" Wynn snapped.

"You may think that, but I put in a lot of hard work to be where I am. I know you're capable. Just relax and reset. Keep trying. Anger is our enemy," Akara said.

Wynn took a deep breath and another. "I should meditate awhile before I try again."

"Take your time," Akara said and turned towards me. "Maximilian, I think it's time you work on an advanced project."

"Like what?" I replied.

Akara beckoned with her finger to go inside the house. We stepped down to the basement, which was a surprisingly large storage room. She opened a tremendous shelf and gathered objects into a sack. Waving her hand over the burlap, she made it hover in the air, and we went back outside.

"I think you're ready." Akara smiled as she turned the bag upside down, which spilled out the remains of a large animal. "Summon a unicorn, please."

"You're joking." I chuckled. "It's like the hardest challenge there is for a necromancer."

"I'm aware, but it's also the closest experience I can give you to practice the bone-crushing curse."

"You're about to teach me the bone-crushing curse?"

"Yes, it's necessary for you to master it. Now, listen carefully; the bone-crushing curse is a different incantation than the summoning one, and it takes a little longer to memorize. Still, in my opinion, that's the easiest part. The tricky part is navigating the mental gymnastics required for the bone-crushing curse.

"For the bone-crushing curse, your target must be completely still, or they must be in one focused area with little movement. Next, you say the incantation and perform a traditional palm stab. Now, that's when you feel a mental shove in your head, which the unicorn remains will give you. It's a shove that will try to knock you off balance through a variety of techniques: nausea, vertigo, ear-splitting pain, and the inevitable mental image of a solid black cube. That cube is called necromancer's block."

"Wow, I've never experienced that before," I said.

"It only happens for the more challenging spells. That black cube will try to envelop all of your imagination. Its goal is to leave you thoughtless and push you away from the magic. It's key to focus on what's real. Focus on your hands, your knife, and your target. Your eyes may never leave your target, and most importantly, you must have the incantation memorized like the back of your hand. Let's give this some trials; summon the unicorn," Akara instructed.

I nodded. *"Bones are vessels of the soul. I give my blood to bring life as toll. Rise within and become my companion. Awaken and rise, reform and mend. Become one, once again."*

I followed all of Akara's directions, and just as the knife glowed white at the tip, a black cube trucked through my imagination, buckling my knees and making the world spin. I collapsed to the ground. My whole body felt numb. Betty came up to my side, nudging her head against my neck.

"It's okay, I'm all right," I uttered, my sense of touch slowly restoring. "I wasn't quite expecting THAT."

"You had to experience it for yourself. Get up and try again. It's not an easy summon. But like I said, it's the closest practice you can have to the bone-crushing curse without actually crushing any bones," Akara said.

"Got it."

I tried for the rest of the day, but nothing ever formed. Each time, that black cube invaded my mind, knocking me off balance. It took me a half-hour to regroup before each attempt. The three of us took a break for dinner, and then I went back outside until nightfall, trying to assemble the remains of the unicorn. It never ended up happening that day, but I started getting used to the movement of the necromancer's block.

The following week went by. Wynn and I discussed at dinner how we felt like we were making gains even though we had yet to put anything into fruition with our newest challenges.

"That's all right," Akara assured us. "I think we still have some time left to hone our abilities. I think the two of you should take a night off and relax. I know I could use a night reading and resting. Should you need me, I'll be in my bedroom."

It was raining that evening, hard enough where I didn't want to go outside, but gentle enough to make for the perfect white noise for falling asleep.

I lay on my bed by my lantern, reading a book on the necromancer's block. I thought it might help me in conquering my challenge, but I wasn't learning much. It was more theory-based. It talked about other magic. I found a memory curse rather interesting, but I had never heard of it before. I could make someone forget something they had witnessed, but I would have to be really powerful and advanced.

Knock. Knock. Knock.

"Betty?" I perked my head up.

The door cracked open, and Wynn stepped inside.

"Betty knocks on your door?" Wynn asked.

"Occasionally, a lightning storm will frighten her, and she'll want to lay next to my bed." I sat up.

"Ah, that's really cute. I hope I'm not bothering you," she said.

"Not at all. This book is kind of boring." I chuckled. "How are you?"

"Going a little stir crazy. And I had something on my mind I wanted to talk to you about."

"I'm all ears."

Wynn paused and looked at the ground. "I feel bad that I've been a little rude to you since you've started staying here."

"Don't worry, I haven't gotten that impression at all," I said with playful sarcasm.

Wynn looked up at me. "I'm not always mean. So, don't think I'm a mean person. I can be fun. But no one would really know since I haven't had much of a chance to be fun."

"I wish I could help you somehow."

"Did you know that Akara has a talisman that will take you back to Nezura? I think she has a few of them, but it won't take you back to this island, or at least I don't think. I don't remember. But we could totally sneak out if we wanted to, have a night on the town, and go out drinking and mingling with other people."

"While that does sound very glamorous, my experience with going out on the town has only been drinking alone. It's not that fun. People don't really mingle with other strangers."

"That's unfortunate." Wynn frowned, then smiled. "But I would. I would make a conversation with you if I saw you sitting at a table by yourself."

"I don't know if you would; I was a nobody in Nezura. Just a loser."

"Yeah, yeah, yeah, you've gone on all about that plenty of times. I'm sure that's not true."

"But it is, and to be frank, I don't want to relive those days." I sighed. "What was your life like?"

Wynn folded her arms and leaned against the wall, eyeing the seat at my desk. I motioned for her to sit down, and she smiled as she slid across the floor, plopping down on the chair. "I don't want to bore you with my life story, but I'll tell you a little bit. I suppose it's similar to yours. Not much happened. Had a relatively normal life as a necromancer growing up in Nezura. My parents lived on the west side, and they always thought it was strange how the abilities going through school never really came to me. They definitely worried about my future."

"Boy, do I know that feeling. Sorry, don't mean to interrupt."

Wynn shrugged. "It's all right. Anyway, I was in their small house one day when my dad was having a hard time getting a fire started for a roast. It was for the Nezluma."

"My favorite holiday." I smiled.

"I was around twelve years old, and for some reason, it just felt natural for me to start the fire with my fingertips. It never happened before, but at that moment, I realized there was something different about me because I told my mom I sparked the fire and showed her. That's when she took me to the Noble Necromancers and yada yada yada. Akara told my family she'd have to take care of me forever, and then it was a long, bizarre, emotionally painful process." Wynn sighed.

"So, you've been living here since you were like thirteen?"

"No, I started living here when I turned eighteen. Before that, I had been living with Akara. I was known as her assistant, and my life as the Vyrux was a secret, until one day, another person saw me, and my parents blew my cover. It's a long and stupid story. Basically, another family member saw me with Akara out in public one day, which was a dumb decision, but I had begged Akara to let me go out for my birthday. Anyway, it raised some controversy. But it was all taken care of, I guess." Wynn shrugged.

"Well, when this is all over, maybe we can lead the lives we want to live. I think we've earned it based on our history alone," I said.

"I certainly hope so." Wynn smiled. "Promise me!"

"I promise." I nodded.

"No, that's not good enough. You have to pinkie promise!" Wynn held out her pinky in front of me, which, of course, I locked.

Twenty-two years earlier…

Mozer was reading a thick text titled "Conquering War" in his room. He sat at a desk underneath an arched window with a broad view of Lavarund from the third floor of the royal castle. He studied each page. It was his fifth time reading it through. Though it was once mandatory reading by his father, he grew to appreciate the vicious imagery, the battle strategies, and how to instill fear in your enemies. Memorization would be necessary. Mozer figured if he were in a predicament, he wouldn't go off instinct but rely on the lessons he learned in "Conquering War." It was his father's favorite book, but Mozer made sure he would read it more than his father.

Knock. Knock. Knock.

"Come in." Mozer turned in his seat to lock eyes with Lara.

"Prince Mozer," Lara said.

"Yes?"

"Your father would like to see you downstairs."

"What do you mean downstairs? I'm on the third floor. That could mean the second floor, ground floor, or basement."

"Basement chamber."

Mozer paused for a moment, and the corner of his lip curled up. "Take me, please. It's been a while since I've been down there." Mozer's voice was a slithery whisper.

Lara hid her grimace, but she couldn't hide her goosebumps. "Yes, I can take you down."

The two of them walked side-by-side through the castle's corridors, and Mozer scanned Lara's body up and down. She could feel his leer without looking over. The walk couldn't finish fast enough for Lara. When they reached the basement, Lara stopped at the bottom of the steps and pointed at the end of the hall.

"Thanks." Mozer's crooked lips curved up, and he strolled down and entered the chamber. Walking down the aisle of cellars, he saw his father at the end with his arms folded, waiting outside an iron door. "Father."

"My prince. How old are you now? Fifteen?"

Mozer sneered. "You don't know the age of your only child."

His father smacked him across the face.

"You called me down here just to hit me?" Mozer smirked.

His father narrowed his eyes. "No. That's for getting smart with me. I've called you down here because today marks an important day for you. Your graduation." His father took the sword harnessed on his back and gave it to Mozer.

"Graduation?" Mozer asked.

His father grinned. "Go ahead, I'm done with the man in there. I'll see you for dinner, and when I check back later this evening, he better not be moving. If you graduate, I'll specially gift you a sword crafted to your liking. Whatever size, shape, or material you want. Hell, we can even disguise it in a cane. How's that sound?"

Mozer gulped. Mozer knew this day would come soon, but he didn't know when. Sweat beads covered his forehead and down the rest of his body.

"Don't disappoint me now." His father scowled.

"You're not going to be here after I'm done?" Mozer asked.

"You want a vlarking hug? You know what to do." His father stormed out, shoving Mozer's shoulder on his way. "Just get it done!"

"I don't know how!"

His father strode toward the exit and spun around when he reached the other end. "You've seen it before!" His father slammed the door on his way out.

Mozer stared ahead and yanked open the handle, entering the cellar to find a man with his wrists chained up against the wall. Mozer unsheathed the sword and approached the man, quivering. The man had a sunken face with white-hair and deep wrinkles that could be mistaken as scars. His rib cage was completely visible.

"So you're just going to kill me without knowing a thing about who I am?" the old man said with a surprising amount of life left in him.

Mozer tightened his lips and his grasp on the handle of the sword.

"I could make you more powerful than your father, you know."

Mozer inched closer.

"I'm not trying to hold on to life. You'd have to be daft if you thought I'd have a shot at survival."

Mozer didn't reply.

"Your father is a vlarking idiot, and I could make you more powerful than he could ever imagine."

Mozer cocked the blade behind his back, ready to give a clean slice.

"But if you kill me, you'll always live in the shadow of your father—mark my words. You can read 'Conquering War' all you want, but the information I have could stop your father and give you the crown you earned. You could kill him with the power of your mind if you really desired. And who knows, I might regret this someday, but it's a roll of the dice, for we're heading towards inevitable war no matter what, and it will likely fall on your shoulders."

Mozer stopped and rested the tip of the blade on the stone floor. "What the vlark are you talking about?"

"You can learn a way to crush a man's bones without even having to lay a finger on him." The old man grinned. "It's difficult magic, but anyone can identify as a necromancer. Everyone is capable of the power. How well you can concentrate and how fearless you are will only add to your power. Your father is afraid of us because he knows deep down that we are more powerful. Do you fear your father?"

Mozer hesitated.

"I thought just as much. Let me teach you what I know of necromancy. Let me tell you where you can find a book to learn the history of our world and where you can learn spells and curses."

Mozer's eyes widened.

"I can feel your energy," the old man said. "I can even get a glimpse of your mind, and I feel nothing but that damned 'Conquering War,' which is a fine read, but it will only get you so far. You're a talented young man who's capable of incredible power. Kill me. I really don't care anymore, but I'd love to see you take down your father. I can feel the hunger you have to overthrow him."

Mozer trembled.

"That's right. It could be our secret, and I'll be dead. He'll never know how you became so powerful. I'll even beg you to kill me to make this whole process easier."

Mozer stared at his sword and looked back into the old man's widened eyes.

"I'm gonna die anyway. I may as well part my knowledge to you. Your father reminds me of my old man, and if I could, I would've shown my dad who's really the boss."

"Fine." Mozer dropped the sword, which jingled as it hit the ground. "You vlarking bastard. Tell me everything you know, but just be aware, I'm still going to kill you."

"Of course. I understand, nothing personal. It's just business. I've had it comin' anyways, been looking forward to it, really." The old man chuckled.

"You necromancers really are twisted." Mozer shuddered.

"No. I'm just a man who's got nothing to lose."

✖ ✖ ✖

The present...

As the months dragged on, Mozer traveled to the Navy post east of Lostonia once a week. He demanded all guards stay outside as he locked the doors and performed his "inspection."

Mozer would stand in front of an area and say, *"Bones are vessels of the soul. I give my blood to bring life as toll. Rise within and become my companion. Awaken and rise, reform and mend. Become one, once again."*

Only to assemble a handful of pieces of a specific area.

Over the months, he had connected the tail, legs, arms, and head. Mozer only had to affix all the parts to the body.

Standing in front of the behemoth, he said the words, stabbed his palm, and deftly dodged the necromancer's block. The sheer will and concentration made Mozer collapse each time. An hour passed before he opened his eyes and pulled himself up. Mozer admired his latest achievement.

The arms and legs were attached to the body.

If only I had the energy to connect the rest, Mozer thought.

As Mozer left for his thirty-six horse carriage, Holtmeyer met him in the stables.

"Your Highness, may I speak with you for a moment?"

Mozer grumbled. "Talk to my assistant." A piercing pain lingered in Mozer's head after each summoning effort. He slumped into the carriage and slammed the door shut, reaching for a bottle of mead in the cabin.

Lara stood by the carriage during Mozer's entrance, and she approached Holtmeyer. "Is everything all right?" she asked.

"I'm not sure. I've been checking in on the remains after Mozer's visits, and each week, I've noticed more of them are attached to each other. Will you let him know that? None of my men have gone near it, and it's damn near fully assembled," Holtmeyer said.

"In case you haven't figured it out, he's the one assembling them."

"But why?"

"I don't really know. He said something about defending against necromancers, but I'm not sure I buy it."

"Vlark, I was hoping you'd have some more information. I don't even know what those remains are. Is it some kind of prehistoric monster whale with wings?"

"Your guess is as good as mine." Lara sighed. "Definitely prehistoric if I had to guess. Apparently, he's been saying some weird things in his sleep, too."

Holtmeyer arched his brow, taking a moment to pause before saying something he might regret. "May I ask how this is relevant?"

"Please, I know you don't like him. Believe me, you're not alone," Lara assured.

A half-smile pulled up the corner of Holtmeyer's lips.

"It's relevant, though, because he's been talking about some battle taking place at Nezura," Lara said.

"So, war is happening. It's finally happening?"

"I don't know. This is what his girlfriend told me. He blabbers on in the middle of his sleep about a battle in Nezura. I just wanted to give you a warning that we might be mobilizing in the near future."

Holtmeyer clenched his fist. "But that would be so…"

"It's all right; you can say it. I promise, this stays between us."

"Irresponsible!" Holtmeyer yelled in an angry whisper. "The last time the necromancers stormed the kingdom, so many Silver infantrymen died! The necromancers have the Southeast, and things are fine. Why must we sacrifice more men for a needless battle?"

Lara nodded. "I agree. I don't think it's right, but I do have a question for you. Is there any way to observe what's happening in the storage house when Mozer goes in?"

"There isn't."

"Could you make that a possibility?"

Holtmeyer's jaw dropped. "Uh, I think so. Yes."

"Keep this strictly between you and me. Until then, take care, Holtmeyer." Lara turned around and waved, climbing inside the royal carriage.

"What the vlark was that all about?" Mozer gulped his mead.

"Holtmeyer noticed that pieces of bone are starting to connect together, and he wanted to confirm with you that his men aren't touching the remains," Lara said.

"He dared to say that?" Mozer snarled.

"Relax. I told him the truth, that the bones will be put on display and treated with a special process that's important for defense against the necromancers."

"Good. Vlarking idiots." Mozer sneered as the thirty-six horses galloped out of the stables.

As more time passed, I felt like I would have gone insane if it wasn't for Wynn's company on the island. Betty kept me calm, too, but my friendship with Wynn was special. Every morning, she smiled and greeted me. Compared to when I first arrived, it was like I didn't exist.

"When this is all said and done and we defeat King Mozer, we should become triple monarchs and rule over Lavarund with gentle care. We're going to usher in a period of tranquility, the likes of which Lavarund has never seen," Wynn said one morning during breakfast.

Akara listened with a smile, and I nodded along.

"Sounds like a great plan to me," I said.

"And then maybe we'll build three castles! One for me, and one for you, and one for Akara. Whatever design you want, all the bells and whistles. Your dream home. Akara, if you want to have a castle made of nothing but bones because you're a necromancer goddess, go for it!" Wynn beamed. "And mine will be a kingdom of love with bright colors everywhere!"

"Settle down there. While that does sound fun and charming, we have greater things to worry about right now. I still need to see you fly, and I need to see you—" Akara pointed at me. "—summon a unicorn."

"Let's do it. I think I have this under control. I think today might be the day!" I finished up my eggs and pancakes and stormed out the door, carrying the burlap sack of unicorn remains. I emptied them out in front of the grass and felt an extra pep in my step. The daydream of leading Lavarund as king excited all my senses.

Standing in front of the remains, Betty raced over to me from inside the house. I gave her a pat on the back.

"Thanks for joining me."

I focused my attention back on the bones. Whispering the incantation, I locked in my focus. The knife blade became white-hot, and I stabbed my hand. No sting or surge, just an outpour of blood raining down on the ivory.

The necromancer's block invaded my imagination, but I had complete control, like a puppeteer. I imagined the block shrinking until it was nothing more than a pebble. The bones glowed with white light, and they strung together, forming the elusive unicorn.

My jaw dropped, and I fell down. Wynn and Akara sprinted out of the house and gawked at the tall, horned stallion. Betty ran in circles around me.

"Maximilian!" Akara sprinted to my side and helped me back up. As soon as she did, the remains of the unicorn fell back to the ground.

I was drawing in deep breaths. "What happened? Why…did it…collapse?"

"It didn't like you very much." Akara smirked.

"What? Why?" I cried.

"Relax. I'm only teasing. It's good to have a joke every once in a while with so much seriousness afoot. But the summon collapsed because it takes a lot of energy from the caster to keep it sustained. It's not like Betty, where you can summon her and leave her be. The unicorn drains your power, fast."

"Huh, so when you summoned it, it fell apart as well?"

"Mine lasted a little longer than yours." Akara winked.

Wynn ran over to the beach's edge and put her feet in the water, concentrating for a moment. Akara, Betty, and I watched as she turned her back to us. A shot of wind blasted out from her heels, and Wynn reached one hundred feet in the air. She sputtered for a moment, trying to balance. I thought she might fall, but she adjusted until she skated on the air.

"WOOOOO!" Wynn screamed throughout the sky, zigzagging high above the tiny island.

I couldn't look away. My face hurt from smiling so tight. When I glanced over at Akara, she was beaming, as tears ran down from her eyes in rivers.

Later that evening, Akara pulled me aside to the edge of her beach, as far away from the house as we could be.

"I can't tell you how proud I am. You've made tremendous progress since you've been here," Akara said.

"I guess you can thank my mentor for that." I smiled.

"You don't give yourself enough credit. Regardless, I wanted to give you something for what you've done today." Akara dug in her pocket and pulled out an artifact crafted by osseous steel. It had similar features to a knife, but it wasn't. She handed it to me. "You deserve this."

I studied it for a moment. It was scratched and chipped, but I could still see three tiny skulls engraved in the center. Its sides stretched like a rib. It was cut with symmetrical lines and shapes stemming from the middle, showcasing the grandeur of the three tiny skulls. Something about it gave me chills, not because it was intimidating, but I sensed a resonating power from within. "What is this?"

"A crown from Princess Nezalon. The woman who founded Nezura and turned it into the self-sufficient, beautiful city."

My skin tingled all over my body. "I don't deserve this."

"That's how I felt when I received it. But truth be told, she had numerous crowns, all of which are housed in a museum in Nezura. One of the Nobles had this one as a family heirloom, but it's in pretty rough shape. It doesn't contain any magical properties," Akara said.

"It certainly feels powerful, like it's imbued with something."

"I think that probably comes from the art and the sheer age of the crown. It's about a thousand years old. But it was given to me by the Nobles before I invaded the Royal Lavarund castle."

"Why did they give it to you?"

"They knew I would make it to the castle. And I think they wanted to make a statement that our dead crown made it through the walls of the tyrannical king's home. A fact that would drive the Mozer and the Silver Army mad. They'll probably never know because I had it in my possession the whole time as a charm, but our leaders in Nezura knew, and I think that gives them enough satisfaction."

"You sure you want me to have it?"

"With whatever is about to come, I couldn't think of a better person to own it."

"Thank you," I replied.

"Besides, our chances of success increase if I give this to you."

I blinked as my eyes widened.

"Come on, let's go inside," Akara said, stepping towards the house. "Or you can stay out here a little bit longer if you'd like; it's a nice evening. I, for one, am hungry for dinner."

"Yeah, that sounds good," I said and followed her. I put the crown in my pocket.

A bell jingled inside the rustic bookstore. The walls were lined with shelves piled high with texts—tired spines on every faded book. The aroma of aged pages filled the air.

One gentleman was exchanging coppers with an old woman at the counter.

"I'll be with you in a moment," the old woman said, putting on a pair of spectacles and noticing the tall, cloaked figure standing at the front of the store.

The gentleman shuffled outside, and the cloaked figure chained up the doors.

"May I ask what this is about?" the old woman said, gripping a concealed sword under the counter.

The cloaked figure turned around and marched up to the old woman. "I need you to give me a book that's not on the shelves."

"Well, excuse me." She grumbled. "Reveal yourself, and maybe I could understand you better."

The veil dropped, and the old woman recognized her at once.

"You-Your Hi-Highness? Is it r-really y-you? Th-the royal g-guard?"

"Yes, I need you to give me a text on necromancy, specifically a history, if possible," Lara said.

The old woman's jaw dropped.

Lara sighed. "You're not in trouble, and you'll be safe. I'm going to need you to swear to secrecy because I need that book, and I know you have it."

The old woman grabbed a candle burning on the counter. "Follow me." She led Lara to a hall that went downstairs. The basement was lit with a faint blue glow from the luminous mushrooms on the walls. There was a thin layer of fog on the floor as they strolled through aisles of dilapidated shelves.

"Are these all necromancer books?" Lara asked.

"Yes, some areas are different from others. You have spells, recipes, and so forth." The owner stopped in an aisle and pulled out a book from the shelf. "You're going to want this one, *A Necromancer's History*."

Lara smiled and gave the owner a handful of gold coins.

"But, Your Highness, this is way too much! This book is just a fraction of what you're giving me."

"For your trouble."

The old woman blinked and said, "But h-how?"

"I beg your pardon?"

"How did you know about my store?"

Lara paused. Memories of her childhood came rushing back to her.

Oh, how different we'd end up being, but how was I to know? We were kids. But we'd always be family even though it had been years and years. One thing was for certain; this was the shop he told me about.

"My brother, he was a necromancer," Lara said, fighting back the tears, but memories of him being screamed at by her family conquered her mind.

The bookstore owner rubbed Lara's arm and pulled her in for a hug as tears flowed down Lara's face.

"What's his name?" the owner asked.

"Telyos." Lara hiccuped.

"I beg your pardon?" The owner's eyes widened, and Lara repeated herself. "You don't say? He's become a leader now, y'know?"

Lara's jaw dropped.

Mozer sat in his private flagstone chamber, lit up by a fireplace. Across from him was a purple velvet couch that could seat six people, but it only occupied two lovers locking lips and tongues.

Lara stood in the corner of the room by the window in case any invaders were crafty enough to reach the fourth-floor turret, but once Mozer's entertainment reached a certain point, she would desire to depart.

"You may head off to bed, Lara," Mozer uttered, breaking his attention from the couple that started undressing each other. Mozer chugged his mead, spilling some on the side of his face.

"Goodnight, Mozer," Lara said, leaving the room as the king continued watching. She jogged on her tiptoes through the flagstone corridors until she reached her quarters.

She pulled out the key from her pocket, reached under her bed, and opened an iron vault containing *A Necromancer's History.*

Flipping through the pages and scanning the paragraphs for an hour, she came across images of a monster called "The Zevolra," and reading about it gave her chills. There was no doubt that those were the bones Mozer had obtained.

The words faded into fuzz, and the book flew away in the wind. Lara was in the middle of a field, rushing towards a city glistening on the horizon. A unicorn stared at her, nodded, and galloped towards the skyline. Lara knew she had to chase after it. Happiness and hope were promised ahead. Something that wouldn't just affect her, but everyone. It was freedom and compassion, which felt like attainable objects because of the unicorn.

Lara woke up to warm light spilling on her face. Her eyes opened, and she felt well-rested. She jumped out of bed, recognizing that the book was still lying on her lap. Lara stashed it away in her iron box and scanned the floor, looking for any clues that someone had come in. It wasn't uncommon for Mozer to check in on her in the middle of the night. There were no impressions or markings of any kind on the floor. She took a relieved breath and headed down to the stables to prepare another journey to the Navy outpost.

Through the week, Wynn skated in the sky every day, looking smoother with each flight. Akara set up hovering wooden targets over the water for Wynn to blast with fireballs as she flew around.

For once, I was taking it easy by playing fetch with Betty on the beach.

"Are you ready for your final part of your last lesson?" Akara asked.

"Of course!" I beamed. Betty came back and dropped the stick at my feet.

"Memorize this scroll." Akara unraveled a roll of parchment.

The Bone-Crushing Curse
Death comes to those innocent and guilty
I concoct the spell of greatest responsibility
It should never be the first, always the last
Resort. Contort. Crush. And demolish.
Or a structure no more can prosper
The only method I should foster
It can break barriers or walls
But its intent is always for all
Unity.
Toting the thin line
Of death and life
I take in, I ensure,
Virtue in my conjure
I wet my brush in death's goblet
But this paint will create beauty in life.
This paint will create beauty in life.

"Wow, uh, that's some intense stuff," I uttered. There was more information at the bottom.

Instructions:

It is imperative your subject remains still or relatively still. You must focus on your subject every moment. During the words "I wet my brush in death's goblet," your knife should glow a dark red, and that's when you stab your hand. As you impale your hand, say the last two lines.

"How do you feel about it?" Akara asked.

"I think I can do it, might be a little tricky not being able to practice the words and motions on someone."

"I trust you can memorize it and make it happen. We can even trade knives again if you really want." Akara winked. "I'd love to have your knife again."

I smiled. "I think I'll hold on to my own. Thanks, though."

One night, after Akara, Wynn, and I finished up dinner, we were about to relax for the evening in our rooms when Akara's expression soured.

"We need to talk," Akara muttered.

"What about?" I asked. Even Betty picked her head up from lying on the ground.

"You sound so serious." Wynn shivered. "More so than your usual teacher voice."

Akara feigned a smile. "My dreams have been filled with nothing but storms lately. It's just me sitting outside during heavy rain, red lightning crawling over the clouds like a centipede."

"That doesn't sound so bad. I have nightmares where the Silver Army is after me, and I can't shoot out wind or fire. Now that's scary," Wynn said, and an awkward pause lingered.

"I think something is coming. I thought I would know more, but this future is obscured with uncertainty. Just keep on your heels, and watch closely for any omens," Akara said.

"What do you think is coming?" I asked.

"Something evil."

My skin tightened with goosebumps, and all my hairs stood on end.

A week later, King Mozer woke up before the sun greeted the castle. He stared at himself in his vanity mirror that extended up the vaulted ceiling. A twisted grin crept up his face. Mozer stormed out of the hall.

The doors to Lara's room swung open just as she was lying in bed, locking up her iron chest.

"Good morning." Mozer grinned.

Lara's heart thumped in her neck like a bass drum. She stared back at Mozer and smiled, tucking the iron vault under her covers.

"Whatcha got in there?" Mozer inquired.

"Just a book," Lara said in a low voice.

"And you have it stashed in that box?"

"Sir, I don't have a bookcase, nor a nightstand."

Mozer scanned the room from left to right and took a deep breath. "Yeah, you don't have much in here. We ought to fix that. Perhaps later today, but we have more pressing matters to tend to. Are you ready to go to the outpost?"

"Of course."

When the royal carriage entered the Navy outpost, Holtmeyer stood guard by the door to the storage house. Mozer sprinted up to him and grinned, which was Holtmeyer's cue to leave. Once Mozer slipped inside, Holtmeyer went to the stables. Lara sat in the royal carriage, and she beckoned for him. They met inside the cabin.

"He's in there. I figured out a way to peek inside without him knowing," Holtmeyer said.

"I don't know how I feel about it," Lara said.

Holtmeyer's jaw dropped.

"I mean, yes," Lara defended, "I think we should spy on him, but I'm sensing something is going to happen."

"Like what?"

"I don't know. I've been having these visions lately in my sleep. Something's going to happen today."

"Well, why don't we confirm what's going on?" Holtmeyer held out his hand to Lara.

"Do you have a group of men that would follow your orders over the king's?"

"Why yes, I'm confident that every single one of them would."

"That's good because I think we're going to need your forces and my forces combined."

"Lara." Holtmeyer pursed his brow. "Do you mind telling me what the vlark is going on?"

"Let's go check on Mozer."

Holtmeyer rubbed his chin and debated if he should continue to ask. He sighed. "Fine." Holtmeyer climbed out of the cabin, and Lara followed. He took her upstairs to a wooden closet filled with armor, weapons, rope, and nets. "Check out what I've done up here." Holtmeyer guided Lara to the end of the room with a tiny hole poked through the wall. "Take a look."

"That's the size of a small nail. How can I possibly expect to see anything?" Lara said.

"Take a look," he repeated.

Lara put her eye to the hole and saw a wide landscape angle of the storage house. "I'm impressed," she murmured.

"I put together a series of microscopic lenses to get that view," Holtmeyer said.

Lara could see Mozer standing front and center of the massive remains.

"Oh my, he's pulling out a knife. It's glowing brightly. He just stabbed himself in the palm!" Lara narrated. "The bones on the head and neck are attaching!"

"You must be joking!" Holtmeyer whispered.

"He's a necromancer! I knew it!"

Holtmeyer blinked. "Well, it makes a lot of sense now."

"He's just fully summoned the remains of the Zevolra!" Lara wanted to look away and talk to Holtmeyer, but she had to watch every moment.

"Zevolra?" Holtmeyer said. "What's that?"

"A prehistoric monster that used to have flesh and created the Earth or something."

"What the vlark? What's happening now?"

"The neck just connected to the head, and it—"

A deep bellow boomed from the storage house that shook the entire structure of the Navy outpost. Lara's body vibrated.

"What the vlark was that!" Holtmeyer yelled.

"The Zevolra. It's been summoned, and now Mozer is glowing white!"

"Let me see!"

Lara pulled away, and Holtmeyer peeped through the hole, gasping. "Not only is he glowing white, but he's also hovering through the air."

He backed away and let Lara stare through, and she saw Mozer floating towards the massive skeleton. A crown of bone spears enveloped Mozer at the top of the Zevolra's head. It screeched as it spread its sparse bone wings and bent its knees. The Zevolra launched itself through the roof, and the outpost quaked. Wood, iron, and rain poured through the hole. Holtmeyer and Lara tumbled. They waited in silence before the ground settled.

"We have to leave right now! Assemble your men!" Lara screamed.

Mozer cackled until tears streamed down his face as he flew through the air in his cage of bones. The clouds assembled in dark gray armies across the horizon as rain and lightning followed behind. A bright white aura flowed from Mozer.

A new power awakened deep inside his core.

I can stretch out these wings, and no one can see a thing! But I can see them through the rain as if it's clear skies! I feel invincible! The memory spell has activated; no one will ever know! No one will ever know, he thought.

Mozer howled through the swath of storms.

I was relaxing all evening, talking with Wynn and petting Betty in the living room. After another day spent summoning the unicorn remains, I was exhausted. After my first successful attempt, I kept trying it again and again. I only summoned it successfully one more time. It required the right amount of concentration and precision. If something were off the slightest bit, the necromancer's block would knock me like a boulder.

At 8 PM, I was lying in bed with Betty resting next to me when a tap at the door cracked it ajar.

"Come in," I called out. Betty lifted her head up.

"Hey, am I bothering you?" Wynn asked.

"Not at all."

"A thought crossed my mind, and I wanted to ask you something." Wynn took a seat at my desk.

"Yeah, what is it?"

"What do you hope happens after all this?"

I paused for a moment and smirked. "To be honest, I don't know what 'all this' is. Akara selected me to be here, and I still don't know what evil we're going up against."

"It's King Mozer," Wynn said without hesitation.

"Yeah, but are the three of us expected to take him out? Mozer and the Silver Army? I don't want war, but believe me, I want Mozer gone."

"I guess we'll have to see, but we're an integral part of the process." Wynn shrugged. "I think we just need to find a way to sneak into the castle and ambush Mozer!"

"Yeah, don't know how we'll do that. But to answer your original question, I just want to go back to Nezura and be recognized and respected as a real necromancer. Show off my skills on the Caster's Court, the big park in Nezura where all the talented 'mancers strut their stuff. But deep down I think I just want to be accepted. That's all. What about you?"

"I wanna be Queen Wynn, I think. Or try to have the normal life I always wanted."

"I have faith one of those two things will happen. Living a normal life is probably the most likely." I chuckled.

Betty lifted up her head as we heard patter on the rooftop.

"It's okay, Betty, it's just rain." I rubbed the top of her nose, but she scrambled up and jumped onto the floor, trembling. "Whoa, something's really bothering her."

"Yeah, it's okay, Betty," Wynn added, but the tapping from the precipitation grew louder.

The door to my room flew open. Akara rushed in, wide-eyed.

"Everything all right?" I said.

"You two need to stay inside." Akara ran up to Wynn and me, giving us each a sapphire talisman. "If I tell you to leave, leave." She reached in her robes, yanked out two scrolls, and gave one to each of us. "Read the letters if—or when—I tell you to leave."

"Akara, what's happening?" I asked.

"You know how to use the transportation talismans, right?" Akara asked.

"Yes," Wynn said. "Spike it on the ground and stomp on it, correct?"

"Great. Now stay inside and keep Betty calm!" Akara sprinted out of the room.

"What the vlark?" I squeaked.

"Let's watch." Wynn chased after Akara, and I followed.

We stared out the living room window. Akara craned her head up at the dark gray sky as it poured buckets of rain.

A deep bellow shook the house, louder than any thunder I had ever heard. Betty wrapped her arms around me and quivered. I rubbed the side of her body.

"Oh no!" Wynn shrieked.

"What the vlark was that?" I blurted.

Wynn pointed at the window, and just barely, I saw the faint traces of a giant ivory monster sailing through the air like a battleship.

I gasped. "Is that the—"

"I think so. Max, this is it." Wynn clutched my shoulder.

"This can't be happening."

Akara spun around and ran inside the house, drenched. "Get out of here with the talismans! Now! One of you hold on to Betty and go!"

"But Akara, what's—"

"Just leave!" Akara slammed the door shut and returned outside.

Wynn and I stared at each other for a moment as I held on to Betty with my left arm and the talisman in my right hand.

101

"Guess we better go," I said. I checked my pockets to make sure I had my knife and Princess Nezalon's crown.

"I wish we could watch!" Wynn said.

"Yes, but there's no time! Are you ready?"

Wynn nodded.

"Three, two, one!" I said, spiking the talisman on the floor at the same moment as Wynn. We both crushed the gem, and it crackled as we stomped. I felt my skin dissolve into nothing.

Akara stood at the center of her island as lightning flickered, rain flew sideways, and palm trees bent backward. The skeletal Zevolra descended from the sky, with King Mozer standing in the bone crown atop the skull, cackling as the monstrosity floated down.

The Zevolra was larger than the island, and half of its body lay down in the water, while the other half lowered its head and retreated the bone cage. Mozer stepped down the slope of the skull as the rain misted.

"Why, I don't believe it. It's so good to see you," Mozer called out, smirking and sauntering forward.

Akara clenched her jaw and tightened her grip on the knife concealed in her robes.

"I legitimately thought you died." Mozer cackled. "I was taking my new pet out here to stretch its wings, and just as I flew over the Bolt Sea, I saw a bizarre fog. And whaddya know, with a closer look, it's your cute little island home!" He stood a few feet away from Akara, glowing with a white, wispy aura. "How did you do it? I must know because I definitely killed you."

"There's a lot about necromancy you don't know." Akara gritted her teeth.

"I was just trying to make conversation. I assume you had a resurrection spell ready to go. I've only heard about it in texts; I didn't think it was possible. So, congrats on the discovery! You've given me hope." Mozer exhaled. "I'm just so glad I found you here so I can kill you again, for old time's sake." Mozer winked.

Akara remained silent as Mozer stepped closer.

"Do you remember what happened the last time we were together?" Mozer asked.

Akara narrowed her eyes.

"I always think about that kiss. I've never kissed someone so powerful. It was beautiful and so satisfying." Mozer leered at Akara up and down. "I've been craving another kiss from you ever since."

Akara ripped out her cracked knife from her robes, but Mozer leaped forward and knocked the blade out of her hand as he gripped her throat. He forced her head closer to his lips, but Akara pulled out another knife with a glowing tip from her robes and stabbed Mozer directly in the chest. He roared as the white aura around him flowed into the blade, which exploded into a million crumbs of osseous steel.

"Go ahead. Finish me off with another bone-crushing curse."

Akara grinned one last time before her world went blank.

Mozer collapsed and took in a few deep breaths. He lay on the grass of the island. "That bitch!" He groaned. "That vlarking bitch! She took my power." Mozer hobbled back to the obedient Zevolra and clambered to the top of the skull. He gripped his chest to soothe the pain that lingered, though the stab wound disappeared. The bone cage erected once again, keeping him safe. "Let's make another stop." Mozer grinned and chuckled weakly.

27

Holtmeyer assembled his troops in the storage house, where a gentle rain spilled from the giant hole in the roof. The three hundred-member regiment stood stunned and silent in front of Holtmeyer and Lara.

"Men and women of this outpost," Holtmeyer started, "you've served your duty better than any other unit in the country. We have some news about our king, which is, well, let's put it this way; the only person in command right now is Lara. And I will let her speak."

Lara took a step forward and shouted, "As all of you know, King Mozer came here each week to this exact storage house investigating the remains. In actuality, he used summoning spells to bring back a prehistoric monster to life. While some of you may not believe it is true, King Mozer is a necromancer. Holtmeyer and I witnessed the beast come to life and fly out of the storage house. We can no longer trust our king, who ushered in an era of hatred and destroyed this outpost. He has abandoned us, lied to us for years, disrespected many of us, and now, we must look to the necromancers for partnership to help save Lavarund!" Lara paused. She expected an outburst of bickering, but they all nodded in reply. Her lips curved upward.

"I know it is hard to believe, and it may seem like a suicide mission, but we must restore our kingdom that Mozer has damaged. We must charge Nezura and aid the necromancers, for Mozer plans to wipe them out completely and enslave the rest of the land. He has created a greater divide between us and them because he knows they're the only ones who can put his power in check!"

"When do we depart?" an infantryman cried out.

"Get your things, for we are leaving right away!" Holtmeyer yelled. "You're either with us, or you stay here!" He followed up with a battle cry echoed by the rest of the regiment.

They departed from the stables and raced towards the royal palace. Lara assembled the guards of the castle and informed them about everything that transpired. Holtmeyer stood by her side to confirm what she witnessed. Lara added three hundred more warriors to their brigade as they took their horses to the Southeast.

Wynn, Betty, and I reappeared in a small loft at the top of a stone building. The residence only had a desk and a bed for one person.

"Where are we?" I asked, gazing at my hands that had disappeared in front of me a moment ago.

"Well, she said this would take us to Nezura, so I assume that's where we are." Wynn shrugged.

"Yes, but where exactly in Nezura?"

"I don't know." Wynn stepped over to the window and pulled back the curtains. "From the looks of it, we're in the southern part of town. I can see the lowered horizon just north of here. Looks like we're on a main road. Some market shops and bars are just below. Wow, it's a pretty good view."

Betty and I leaned forward, and the three of us gazed out at the skyline. Skull Tower was far to our left, and I could see all the other stone buildings and some pillared structures made of osseous steel. My eyes were glued to the Municipality Building's massive dome, always beautiful to look at from afar.

"This is a pretty nice place Akara has here," I said.

"Do you think she's going to be joining us?" Wynn asked, but Betty hung her head.

"I don't know. It seems like Betty might know something. Let's read the scrolls that she gave us. I mean, she made us take them for a reason, right?"

I pulled the scroll out of my pocket and unraveled it.

Maximilian,

If you crushed the talisman, you must be housed in the apartment that I owned in Nezura. Congratulations, you and Wynn are now the owners. Feel free to sell it if you wish and split the earnings or give it to someone in need. Do whatever, it's yours now.

This also means that I've passed away. That's right; I'm no longer alive. I didn't use another resurrection spell. I'm sorry you had to find out like this. Believe me, I wish I had the courage and strength to tell you and Wynn that I knew I would die, but I'm not one for sentimental goodbyes. Not because I dislike showing emotion, but if I had to say goodbye in person, I would second-guess everything and not want to leave you. Also, that future would have been much worse, trust me. Survival would have been meager.

You and Wynn have some time before you face off against Mozer. He's coming to Nezura. I don't know how you'll do it, but you'll have to figure out how to stop him, although one thing is for sure: you have it in you to succeed. Don't doubt it for a second. Take everything you've learned from staying with me and put it to the test.

I understand that you are probably upset with my passing, especially with no warning, but there's something I want you to remember. Whenever you summon a skeleton or pile of remains, a piece of your personality goes inside whatever you're conjuring. Look at it this way, Betty carries on my legacy. She holds one of my most valuable traits. The joyful little girl I always was is what Betty is. To become a Noble Necromancer, I had to develop a tough exterior and a disciplined manner. But deep down, my spirit has always been the young girl who loved everyone and was afraid of loud noises. Just because I was seen as the best around doesn't mean I didn't have my own fears and uncertainties. Perhaps the greatest lesson I've learned through my long life and career in education is that it doesn't take skill to believe in yourself.

Only if you believe in yourself, Maximilian. I'm confident you'll get it done.

Again, I'm sorry you had to find out about my passing like this, but know that you and Wynn meant a lot to me. We've shared some great moments the past few months, and I wish we could have done that longer. You and Wynn were like son and daughter to me. I was never a mother, but you two felt like my children, and I love everything about each of you. Your successes, failures, and quirks make you who you are, and I wouldn't want that to change for the world, which you and Wynn will save.

I love you, Max. Take care of Betty.

One week earlier...

Telyos sat at his desk in his Municipality Building office, catching up on work until the early evening.

Ah, I haven't even checked the mail today, he thought.

Telyos collected a letter from the cubby outside his door. He stared at it for a while, wide-eyed. The message was closed with the purple wax seal from the Royal Lavarund Castle—the sight of the crown impression sent shivers down his spine. Part of him wanted to burn it. Another part of him wanted to see if any other Noble Necromancers had received similar communication. This was the first time in his tenure that he received a letter from the Royal Castle.

A gentle glide from his letter opener cut the envelope. He unfolded the note.

Telyos,

I know it has been far too long since we last talked to each other, but I'm planning to visit soon. Please don't be alarmed. I've never harbored ill will towards you. I keep having dreams of coming to Nezura. Expect me soon, but I'm not sure when. Something horrible is going to happen. What it is, I'm not sure, but I've been having vivid visions, and I know this is my destiny. I'm risking my life sending this letter to you, but I made a friend at the old bookstore you used to visit when we were kids. The bookstore owner knew how to deliver this to you. I'm sorry if the wax seal gave you any worry. I understand if you're skeptical, but to prove I'm serious, I'll risk my life with the following sentence:

I renounce King Mozer and wish his reign to end with his demise.

Such words are punishable by death to write together, especially if the document is signed. Funny, isn't it? How an action so small as moving your wrist with a quill in hand can cause your undoing?

With much love and respect,
Your sister,
Lara

Telyos' heart sank to his stomach, his eyes brimmed, and he dried them off with his sleeve. He sat back in his chair, closing his eyes.

Those bastards. I was ripped away by Silver Infantrymen from my own damn house. Lara's screams in the middle of the night were the last time I heard her voice, he thought.

Later that same evening, Telyos went to the border gate that protected the city with a twenty-foot-high bone wall.

"Hello, Vera," Telyos said as he walked into the central outlook tower.

She jumped. Vera was alone in the stone chamber, sitting on a couch while a skeletal bird stared out through the wall's rectangular slit.

"Telyos." She sat up, saluted, then relaxed her shoulders. "What can I do for you?"

"It's good to see you. It's been a while."

"It really has, yeah, but no news is good news." She shrugged.

"Look, I, uh, don't know how to say this. But if you see anyone who looks like they might be from the Silver Army or anyone from the Royal Castle, get a hold of me immediately. Send a skeletal pigeon or something."

"You're expecting someone from there? Someone trustworthy?"

"Uh, yes."

Vera narrowed her eyes at him. "People from the Silver Army are usually met with our skeletal knights. It's rare, but it has happened. We gotta watch out for spies, y'know?"

"Yes, and I understand it might look strange, but you have to trust me. I think I might know someone who's turned over to our side."

Vera inhaled a deep breath. "All right, I'll keep watch for someone like that and hold off on attacks."

"Thank you very much, Vera." Telyos stepped over and handed her some gold coins. "For your trouble."

Vera's jaw dropped. "Telyos, you really don't have to do this. My goodness."

"Please, I understand it's a huge favor. This person might come in a week, maybe in a few days; I have no idea. But keep watch for them."

"Well, thank you very much, I really appreciate it. One last question, man or woman?"

"Woman."

Tears streamed down my cheeks. Wynn sniffled repeatedly, and Betty nestled her head against my body.

"I can't believe this," I uttered, falling to the ground on my back, gazing up at the ceiling. My mind felt numb and fuzzy, like an emotional hangover.

Wynn sobbed. Time was irrelevant. *Did we sulk for minutes or hours?* It didn't matter. The sun sank regardless.

"No!" Wynn yelled. "Don't you understand, Maximilian, if Akara saw us right now, she'd be pissed!"

I picked my head up. Wynn was lying on the bed next to Betty, but she sat up.

"What do you mean?" I asked.

Wynn opened her mouth to say something but froze, staring in the corner with goggle-eyed wonder. Footsteps echoed from behind me. Betty even sat up and lowered her jaw. I turned around, my skin tightening up.

The ghost of Akara was staring at each of us. I scurried to Wynn. Akara was smiling, the look of a proud mother on her face.

None of us said a word. We just watched her. She was wearing an elegant dress, decorated with bones like a necromancer queen. In her hand was a goblet, and she held it up as if to say, "Cheers."

She took a drink, smiled, turned around, and faded into the wall.

I rubbed my eyes and continued staring at that empty corner.

"Did you see that?" I said.

"Yeah, Betty saw it too," Wynn murmured. We stayed silent for a few moments before she spoke again. "I don't know about you, Maximilian, but in a way, I feel weirdly consoled after that."

"Same. What were you saying earlier about Akara being pissed at us?"

Wynn still held her gaze on the corner. "She'd be pissed because she wouldn't want us to be sad; she'd want us to focus on the task at hand, or vlark, even celebrate now that we're finally off the island. And that vision we just had? That's probably her telling us to get off our asses and get a drink."

I let her words sit in my head for a moment. "You're right. I think that's a good idea. There's a place around this neighborhood I always went to. It's a nice, secluded spot. You down to go?"

"Can Betty come?" Wynn rubbed Betty's back and smiled for the first time in what felt like an eternity.

"Of course." My lips curved up.

"Can I ask you another question?" Wynn tilted her head.

"Sure."

"Why did you leave Nezura in the first place?"

I sighed. "Let's talk about it over some mead."

"Yeah, let's collect our thoughts with a drink. But that's all we have time for, only one," Wynn stated. We walked downstairs to find a furnished living room with a couch, a couple of chairs, and a table.

"This place is bigger than I thought," I said.

"Yeah, not bad. I can't believe we own it. But we'll have to talk about what we want to do with it later," Wynn said.

"Yeah, to be honest, it's the least of my concerns right now."

We went out the door, strolling down Homunculus street. Caster's Court was visible to our right, the stadium-sized park square with trees and greenery encircling it. It even had the country's largest water fountain. Towering over everything at Caster's Court was the statue of Akara perched at the top of the fountain.

"What a view," Wynn whispered as we made our way towards it. We passed by shop owners who had skeletons managing their storefront markets. "I just want to go skipping about! It's so wonderful being immersed in the world!"

"Yeah, we'll have time to celebrate later," I warned.

Wynn spun her neck back and squinted. "I don't see anything on the northern horizon. No sign of Mozer and the Zevolra yet."

"That's good. We should have a decent amount of time on our side still."

People glanced at Wynn as we passed by them since natural hair color was the norm in Nezura. The red streak running down her long black hair drew attention. But so did Betty, as kids were gawking. *"Whoa! What kind of summon is that?" "Can I pet her?" "Wow! I wish I had one!"*

Betty enjoyed the neck scratches and back rubs, but Wynn and I continued moving after a few minutes of socializing.

"I was afraid this might happen," I said. "The bar I always went to is down this block of alleys." I led the way forward, but memories and flashbacks gave me goosebumps.

We walked to the pub with the dilapidated Risers sign. Inside, only one person sat at the end of the bar. Its chairs, stools, and tables were all crafted from ebony wood. The white stone walls looked worn but inviting. The smell of apples, cinnamon, and fermentation hung in the air.

"It's usually pretty quiet and not very busy, one of the reasons I like this place so much," I said, taking a seat at the elbow of the bar where Wynn and Betty joined.

A skeleton working behind the counter turned to look at us.

"Henry, how are you?" I asked.

Henry's teeth curved up. "Max! Is that you? My goodness, it's been forever, huh? Where you been?"

"It's a long story, had to leave town after that one night."

"Yeah, I don't blame you." Henry hopped over the counter and hugged me. "Ryoz and I were really worried about you, pal. Ryoz ain't here, but I know he'd be happy to see you and know you're all right. Sheesh. I was askin' all around town for you. No one knew where you went. And the fact that it happened in my pub, I can't help but feel responsible. So please, for you and your friend, drinks on the house. What would you like?"

"I'll take a mead," Wynn said.

The skeleton rubbed his jaw. "Yeah, what kind? We got metheglin, melomel, pyment, medica."

Wynn glanced at me with uncertainty. "I don't know what any of those are," she whispered.

"We'll take two glasses of melomel." I smiled. Looking back at Wynn, I said, "The melomel is made with blackberries. It's delicious. I never met anyone who didn't like it."

"Sounds yummy," Wynn said.

Henry strolled over to the bar and filled up two glasses of mead. As he came by to drop them off, he stopped. "Whoa, what kind of summon is that?"

"It's a velociraptor," I said. "Her name is Betty."

"Well, golly, I don't reckon I've ever seen a skeletal velociraptor. How beautiful. And who's your friend? Sorry, I didn't introduce myself sooner. I'm Henry."

"Wynn."

They shook hands.

111

"Pleasure." Henry turned his attention back to me. "Again, terribly sorry for what happened last time, just holler if you need anything." He knocked on the wooden bar and spun around to chat with the other customer.

"What was that all about?" Wynn asked. "What happened the last time you were here?"

I took a few gulps of the mead and exhaled a sigh of satisfaction. "The last time I was here was the last time I was in Nezura. It was the straw that broke the camel's back."

I told Wynn all about how I moved to Nezura after what happened to Uncle Leopold. Then I explained my life with the kindhearted Mr. Cole, and when he had passed away, I was alone. I had caught up with Megan every now and then, but she had been a busybody. We had rarely seen each other. Then I told her all about what had happened when I was pummeled at Risers months ago.

Wynn put her hand on my back and rubbed it. Betty even leaned over and nudged my shoulder with the tip of her head. I gazed down at my drink as I remembered everything. Out of the corner of my eye, Wynn traced the tiny scars scattered around my face.

"Did they do that to you?" Wynn held her hand over her mouth.

"No, these cuts came from a lifetime of abusive parents and schoolyard bullies." I sighed, finishing the rest of my mead.

"Oh, Maximilian, I'm so sorry." Wynn hung her head.

"It almost makes me not want to save these ungrateful jerks if given the opportunity." I clenched my hand around my glass.

"Oh, Max, you can't think like that. Not all of them are bad people. Give them a chance. If we save the day, we'll change a lot of minds. You might even inspire all those other kids who are struggling necromancers but want to get better."

"Yeah." I nodded. I knew she was right. "Sorry, I don't really want to think about that stuff too much. We have a lot to focus on right now. This is our new life, and Mozer is the challenge that stands in front of us."

"You're right. I was just thinking about how we should handle this situation, and I have an idea."

"What's that?"

"Let's finish our mead and go straight to the Municipality Building. We still have plenty of time to reach one of the Noble Necromancers. They need to know Nezura is in danger."

"That's a good idea. If there's anyone who would help us, it would be Telyos. Have you met him before?"

"No, I haven't, but I always respected him."

"He's a great guy." I smiled. "Definitely someone who will listen to us."

Wynn and I finished our drinks and left the bar that once felt like my home.

"Leaving already? Have another drink on the house, please!" Henry yelled.

I waved my hand. "Another time! Take care, Henry. Tell Ryoz I said hello."

The three of us headed north to the dome-shaped Municipality Building. Skeletal horses pulled carriages by our side as the town of the dead sprang to life with evening crowds clamoring for entertainment, drinks, and skeletons performing songs on street corners.

Betty drew glances from onlookers, but we didn't stop our stride until we reached the Municipality Building. I gazed at the towering pillars outlining the structure. It was enclosed by a busy circular street filled with people getting ready for their evening plans and buying groceries for the coming week.

"It's so crowded tonight," I uttered.

Wynn and Betty were a few paces ahead of me. "C'mon, Maximilian!" She spun around and waved.

I jogged ahead to catch up with them, and we hopped up the steps until we were inside. The familiar scent of parchment and paper delivered memories. I froze for a moment.

"How may I help you?" the man at the counter asked, furrowing his brow. He had long hair, and his face was void of wrinkles.

"We're here to speak with any of the Noble Necromancers in the building," Wynn said.

"I don't see any appointments on the schedule." He sneered.

"What's your name?"

"Danny."

"Look, Danny, we don't have an appointment, but we don't have a lot of time. This is a dire issue, and we need to speak with one of them," Wynn argued.

"I don't know who you are, but the Noble Necromancers are all very busy. You may as well run along because they can't meet with you. Suppose you're not important enough to schedule a meeting with them. In that case, there are always audience communications during the town hall meetings, so feel free to embarrass yourselves then with your little squabble to the leaders. I bid you a good evening."

Wynn's jaw dropped while my hands tightened into fists.

"I don't think you understand the severity of this situation." Wynn scowled with eyes that could burn.

"Please, explain. This is entertaining." Danny grinned.

"Nezura is going to get wiped out by King Mozer. We have information that we need to get to the Noble Necromancers to issue a shelter in place order or an evacuation of the people. Meanwhile, my friend and I will stop Mozer."

Danny paused before he howled. "That definitely tops the list of one of the most insane things I've ever heard! That's rich. Real rich. Thanks for the chuckle, but if you don't leave now, I'll get security."

"You may as well because we're not going anywhere! We trained with Akara for too long to just get laughed at!"

He laughed until he was blue in the face. "So now you're talking about a dead woman?" He snorted. "You're something else, you know that?"

"So, if I said I was the Vyrux, that would mean nothing to you?"

He took a few deep breaths trying to regain his composure, but he cracked up again. "Whatever you say, lady. I've had my fun. I'm getting security now if you don't leave."

Wynn held out her palm, and a blazing ball of fire appeared from her wrist, expanding closer to Danny's face. I could feel the heat, and I backed away. Danny screamed. Wynn made the fireball disappear and glared back at him. "I told you, I'm the Vyrux."

Danny raised his fingers to his face while the charcoal smell of burnt hair permeated through the lobby. His fingers traced his hairless eyebrows, and he rubbed his freshly bald head.

"What did you do?! Are you vlarking crazy?! Give me back my hair now!"

Wynn cackled, and I couldn't help but snicker too.

"This isn't funny!" Danny screeched.

Wynn continued to laugh as she strolled past the desk, heading towards the main hall. Betty and I ran forward as Danny chased after us.

"Stop right there!" Danny shrieked. "I can have you imprisoned, you know!"

"Ah, I thought of a way to make yourself useful, so I don't burn off anything else on your body." Wynn marched up to him. "Why don't you guide us to one of the Noble

Necromancers? I have a preference to see Telyos. I've always admired his ability, intellect, and the fact that he's a first-generation necromancer."

"Okay! Okay! Just follow me!" Danny scurried ahead, and we followed behind. Not another word was exchanged. We walked up a circular ramp to the second floor, down a hall with high ceilings that echoed our footsteps. As we approached an arched wooden door, Danny said, "Please wait right here," and he knocked.

"Come in," a voice said from the other side.

Danny cracked open the door, but Wynn cut in front of him and squeezed through the entrance first. Danny grunted. *"What the vlark!"* Betty and I followed Wynn.

"Yes? What can I do for you?" Telyos asked with a lifted eyebrow. He was standing over his desk, which was covered with scrolls. "Ah, Maximilian! Good to see you, I think?" He let out a nervous laugh. "What's going on?"

"Hi. I'm Wynn, the Vyrux. These are my friends, Maximilian and Betty, brought together and trained by Akara, but I guess you already know Maximilian. We came to warn you that King Mozer is on his way to destroy Nezura while riding in on the summoned remains of the Zevolra. We thought you should know because we want to save as many people as possible before we fight."

Telyos froze for a lengthy thirty seconds as he glanced between the four of us. Danny stood in the corner with his arms folded. "I'm terribly sorry. They barged their way in here, sir, and uh, well, uh…"

"How can I help?" Telyos said to Wynn.

Danny gaped, Betty tilted her head, and my brow arched.

"So, you believe us?" Wynn replied.

"Yes, I received a letter about a week ago that made me suspicious that something notable would happen soon. Not to mention, Maximilian and I have a history, and I trust him not to waste my time. I just need you to show me your fire, and I'll believe every word you said to me."

"No problem." Wynn held out her hand.

"Uh! May I object? I've already seen it, and she took off all the hairs on my head!" Danny barked.

"And you look great, Danny. I'm sure it was done with good reason. Please, Ms. Wynn, if you don't mind. Before I do anything drastic to protect the people of Nezura, I must see your power. I believe you, but I'm sure you understand."

"Of course." Wynn smirked as another ball of fire blazed from her wrist, growing in size, spinning in the air until we all started to sweat. It shined so brightly and roared so loudly that I closed my eyes and covered my ears.

"Very good! That will be enough!" Telyos hollered, wide-eyed. "You've convinced me. Now we have to face the challenge of convincing the others, which won't be as easy."

As night approached, the lands over Lavarund saw an unexpected downpour the almanacs never predicted. People in villages, farms, and towns stood inside their houses as the roads flooded, gazing up through their windows. They all swore they saw a cackling madman riding the skull of a giant monster flying south.

Telyos alerted all twelve Noble Necromancers. He assembled them in the flagstone meeting chamber towards the back of the building. While it felt secluded, they did have a broad window view over the bustling city streets.

I was standing in front of the room next to Betty, Wynn, and Telyos. All the Noble Necromancers pierced us with glares as they sat at the U-shaped table made of osseous steel. They were between the ages of forty and sixty. Half of them were men; half of them were women. Sweat puddled in the crevices of my arm, bleeding onto my undershirt. I fiddled with Nezalon's crown in my pocket.

"Noble Necromancers, I've assembled you here because Nezura is about to be under attack by King Mozer. I've received information from these two that he's currently heading south," Telyos stated.

"Has Vera been alerted that the Silver Army is coming?" asked Zenzo, one of the oldest Noble Necromancers with thick lenses and a thick white mustache.

"No, she hasn't because the Silver Army isn't coming with the king," Telyos said.

Bickering broke out among them.

"Are you suggesting that Mozer is coming here by himself? That's appalling! Not even he is that daft to make such an attempt," Zenzo said.

"Yes, he's coming here by himself. I know it because I saw him on the move," Wynn said. "I don't think you know the king as well as you think you do." She exhaled. "He's a necromancer who's managed to summon the remains of the Zevolra."

They glanced at each other for a moment before snickering, except for Zenzo, who continued to stare at us.

"I gotta say, this is a good prank to pull right before the holiday weekend, Telyos," said Maya, an older woman with a sharp jawline. "But you're wasting our time."

All of them stood up except for Zenzo. Telyos cleared his throat before he said, "This isn't a prank. This is a real warning. Wynn is the Vyrux. She and Maximilian were, uh…" Telyos took a deep breath. "Wynn and Maximilian were trained by Akara."

A brief silence passed. Everyone's smile vanished.

"Have a good weekend, Telyos." Maya waved as she led the pack of Noble Necromancers towards the doors.

Telyos turned to Wynn and nodded. She held out her palms, and a fireball burst into the air, floating over the table and increasing in brightness and size until they spun around. Their eyes widened. The miniature sun blazed and roared in the middle of the room and then disappeared with the snap of her finger. All of them stared and paused.

"I'm not sure what I just witnessed, but I'm sure there's an explanation." Maya shook her head. "Come now, everyone, it's the end of the day. Let's celebrate the weekend, and we'll see where we're at on Tuesday."

I felt trapped and useless. There had to be something I could do to help. Telyos and Wynn had tried everything. I clenched my jaw, took a deep breath, yanked out Nezalon's bone crown, and held it up in the air. My pulse thumped in my ear, and my mouth went dry.

"This was given to me by Akara after I proved my worth as a necromancer!" I shouted. "She told me one of you gave this to her before she left to storm Mozer's castle!"

Maya gasped and gazed at the crown. She tried to form words but couldn't. It took a moment for her to say, "Akara gave that to you?"

I nodded.

"Everyone, don't leave just yet." Maya approached me and lowered her voice so only I could hear her. "Please explain."

"Akara said that it was symbolic for her to invade the castle with the crown by her side. She gave it to me," I said.

"I thought she died in the castle?"

"Yes, but she performed the resurrection spell. She saw the future play out in between the plane of existence. But I think she's gone for good now, unfortunately."

"I always thought the resurrection spell was a myth, but if anyone could figure out how to do it, it was Akara. May I see the crown?" Maya asked.

I gave it to Maya, and she turned it over in her hands, tracing the designs with the tip of her finger. "I, and the rest of us, owe you an apology. Sorry." Maya turned around, and she announced, "Let's sit back down everyone, our two guests here deserve our assistance."

The Noble Necromancers returned to their seats and gave us their full attention.

"I believe you," Zenzo said, "but did you have a strategy in mind on what we should do?"

"Yes, all of you should shelter in place or evacuate the people. Leave the battle with Mozer to me and Maximilian," Wynn said.

"I'm sorry, but we barely know who you two are. We have to be involved! We are the Noble Necromancers, and we will protect our people!" one of them argued.

"Let us join the fight!" another hollered.

"Yes, I agree," another chimed.

"Enough!" Wynn shouted. "I wish more than anything that Akara was here right now to explain to you all how this is going to happen! We've received the necessary training. This is our battle."

The room went silent. Then, discussions broke out among them, with Zenzo and Maya leading the conversations. Maya explained the conversation she had with me to the rest of them.

"We apologize," Maya said. "We will follow your directions out of respect for Akara's plan. But please forgive our skepticism. This is the first we heard any of this. Akara didn't tell us much about her life."

"She didn't want to," Zenzo added. "Just wanted to be known as the hero of Nezura and Lavarund. I don't even think we know half the spells she could do. Her magic was something else."

All of them nodded and took a moment of silence.

"As far as evacuation and shelter-in-place go, I don't see it happening," Maya said. "It's a holiday weekend, albeit not a major holiday, but most people have Monday to rest, so they're out and about celebrating the Necromancer's Primacy."

"This fight is about to take place on the anniversary of the first recorded necromancer summon, how prophetic," Wynn said. "Well, it's worth a shot to alert the people. We will need space for this battle. Maximilian and I think it would be best to lead King Mozer to Caster's Court. So, please, try your hardest to keep people away from there."

Maya sighed. "We can put up blockades, but the people aren't going to like it."

"Better to have a bunch of angry people than lives lost." Wynn shrugged.

"How long do we have until Mozer's arrival?" Zenzo asked.

"Uh, I think we have a few hours at least. The Zevolra can fly, but it was pretty sluggish."

"A few hours?" Zenzo uttered.

"Oh no, this isn't looking good," Maya said. "If we had a day to prepare, that would be better, but people aren't going to want to lock themselves up or leave with such short notice. They're out there partying like animals!"

"We better make an announcement from Skull Tower now, as we would for emergency weather," Zenzo suggested.

"Good plan." Telyos pointed. "Anything else we should discuss?"

"No, I think it's best if we get a move on," Maya directed.

"Great. I'll make the announcement from Skull Tower," Telyos said. "Wynn, Maximilian, and Betty, I wish you three the best of luck, for it seems our welfare depends on it."

"We'll be up at Caster's Court!" Wynn turned to me and whispered, "Thank vlark that's over. Let's get outta here."

Betty, Wynn, and I jogged out of the Municipality Building. We headed towards the south side of town, where Caster's Court stood over the rest of the city. As we weaved through the bustling crowds of drunks, laughing necromancers, and street performers, people stopped and craned their necks upward.

"I didn't know it was supposed to rain today?" said people among the crowds.

A gentle drizzle came from the sky as clouds thickened by the second. Betty stared at us and lowered her back as if to say, "Hop on."

Climbing on her back, Wynn sat up front, and I wrapped my arms around her. Once we were seated comfortably, Betty sprinted faster than a horse towards Caster's Court.

A horn blew from the top of Skull Tower. Telyos' voice boomed through the streets of the whole city. "Seek shelter immediately or evacuate. Everyone must seek safety for an emergency storm, and a dangerous situation has arrived that's being investigated. Those that stay outside will endanger their lives. Don't panic. You have enough time to get back home, even if it's on the other side of the city. Get home safely. We will announce when it's okay to come out again! The current time frame is unknown for the restrictions. Have food for the next few days in your house. Caster's Court will have a bone-wall around the perimeter and will be strictly off-limits. If you're currently at the park, please leave immediately. I will repeat this announcement as needed."

"It only seems like a gentle rain?" was the sentiment among the conversations we passed, riding on Betty.

Some scurried into their homes, while others continued to party on the streets.

"Should we tell them? Should we do anything?" I asked.

"They're going to figure out soon enough they shouldn't be outside. There's only so much we can do!" Wynn said.

Betty weaved through the skeletal horses on carriages. The smooth stone streets were freckled with puddles. As Betty splashed through them, I shivered. The sun was setting as Betty ran all the way south down Homunculus Street, a wide road with many stone buildings of shops, restaurants, and pubs. As we approached Caster's Court, droves of people were moseying away from the park. However, there were still crowds hanging around, playing sports with their skeletal dogs, cats, and other small animals.

"Everyone, get the vlark out of the way!" Wynn hollered as we entered Caster's Court on Betty's back, but no one seemed to notice us. "Listen to the message, dammit!"

The announcement continued from Telyos at Skull Tower, and all of them stopped and stared north.

"It's only drizzling," one teen protested.

Suddenly, bone spears emerged from the perimeter of Caster's Court.

"Oh vlark, guess we better go," the teenager said to his friends, and all the people jogged away. Some of them shrieked hysterically.

"Good, that takes care of that." Wynn dusted off her hands, and we hopped off Betty's back. "Great job, little dino-girl." Wynn scratched underneath her jaw.

We were in the barricaded park alone. I gazed at the northern horizon; gray clouds obscured the land beyond Nezura. Peering through, I didn't see a flying Zevolra.

"Keep an eye on the sky, will ya? I've never actually read this plaque before," I said to Wynn as I approached the stone tablet in front of the Akara fountain.

This is a fountain devoted to our beloved Akara.

Everything a necromancer should be is what Akara embodied.

She graduated 25th in her class of 300 Necromancers. If you include the other two schools, she probably finished 75th. But that never stopped her from working hard to become one of the most talented necromancers that have ever existed.

She taught at Nezura Tertium at the beginning of her career. And that's where she strengthened her abilities through her educational craft.

When she realized her power had grown significantly in a couple of years, she left Nezura to journey independently and experience life in a necromancer excluded world. This is where she discovered the remains of a unicorn, brought them back to Caster's Court, and did the unthinkable by raising them up in front of a crowd of 40,000.

But her talents didn't stop there. The Silver Army Spy, Kyra, known as the Necro-Hunter, was discovered and defeated by Akara.

Because of her heroics, she became one of the thirteen Noble Necromancers. Around this time, she discovered groundbreaking spells, not just one, but multiple.

Most Notably:

Bone Lance—a magic projectile to shoot at an opponent.

Amplification—a spell that boosts the power of a skeletal warrior.

It's likely she mastered other spells without any record. In which case, they were probably deemed too dangerous for public use.

Her vision was to see necromancers live freely among Lavarund, united with the world outside our metropolis. On her own, she summoned an army of skeletal knights to challenge King Mozer by herself. While she lost her life, her memory will never be forgotten. She was our benevolent leader, and may this fountain keep her memory alive as a pillar of kindness we all strive to be.

"Have you ever read this before?" I yelled over to Wynn.

"No, I haven't," she said, still petting Betty.

"It's a nice write-up. I didn't know about those spell discoveries. Makes you wonder what else she knew."

A loud groan boomed through the air. Squinting at the sky, I saw the silhouette of the skeletal Zevolra. Its massive skull faded in through the clouds, flying closer to Nezura as the rain poured down.

"Looks like this is it!" Wynn shouted with a crazed grin and twinkle in her eye.

"What's the matter with you? Are you excited about this?" I asked.

"Vlark yeah! I love the rain, and also, I wanna flex my Vyrux-ian muscle. This is the plan. I'm going to fly up and hurl some fireballs at him, get a feel for what we need to do, and then I'll lead him towards Caster's Court, and we can take it from there."

"What should I do?"

"Are you serious right now? Akara trained you, but even I know what you should focus on! The bone-crushing curse, dude! She made sure you mastered that, right?"

"Oh, uh, yeah." I nodded, wiping the rain away from my eyes.

"So then try to kill Mozer when he's distracted or going on some long-winded speech. I don't know; we'll figure it out, gotta go!"

"Good luck!" I yelled.

"Bye, Max, should anything happen, just know I love ya, buddy."

"I love—"

Wynn rocketed off the ground with a burst of wind shooting out her heels. She dashed up the air as if leaping up multiple steps at a time.

"You too." I looked at Betty and waved her over. She approached me and tilted her head curiously. "Let me hop on your back again. I could use the ground speed."

She lowered her tail and held her head up proudly.

Mozer cruised towards Nezura. *The City of Ivory,* he thought. *After I'm done, it'll be The City of Dust. Yes, we're going to squash their stupid Skull Tower into rubble, and we're going to demolish the Municipality Building. My beautiful Zevolra. We'll lay down at the east and roll all the way to the west, crushing everything, taking souls as we go along. This tops any birthday celebration I've ever had.*

Whoosh!

The Zevolra bone crown was rattled by a punch of flames in the blink of an eye. Mozer stammered backward but clutched onto the wall of the cage.

"What the vlark was that?" Mozer scanned his surroundings as the Zevolra continued flight as if nothing happened.

Another blast of flames struck the bone crown.

"Dammit!" Mozer flinched, but he stroked a spear from the crown and cracked up. "Go ahead, I know it's you, Vyrux. Keep 'em coming; I can do this all day!"

A fireball smashed against the crown again, and Mozer howled with laughter. "You're good, you know that, you vlarking bitch. Let's kill you first, so I don't have to deal with a pestering fly as I perform my magnum opus."

The Vyrux hovered in front of the bone cage, grinning and winking. "The name's Wynn! Nice to meet ya!"

The Zevolra bellowed a whale-like sound and swung its massive left claw at Wynn, who narrowly dodged the attack in between its talons.

"Gonna have to do better than that!" Wynn shot a fireball at Mozer, exploding against the crown. She cackled through the hammering rain.

Lap it up while you can, Mozer thought. Wynn skated on the air towards Caster's Court. The Zevolra continued to follow, paces behind, but lockstep with Mozer's mental commands. *That fountain looks like the perfect landing spot.*

Wynn cruised through the air like a smooth javelin toss. The Zevolra lagged a decent amount behind as Wynn landed, skipping on the layer of water over the pavement of Caster's Court.

"How'd it go?" I screamed from Betty's boney back.

"I don't know! Mozer's up in a bone crown on top of the Zevolra's head! I hurled some fireballs, but I don't know if it did much. Need to keep trying!"

The Zevolra soared over Nezura. Crowds of people screeched as Telyos repeated, "Everyone keep calm! The situation is in the right hands!"

Betty ran towards Wynn without my command and trembled. She grabbed Wynn with her boney arm and dragged her further away from the fountain.

"What's the big idea, Max?" she asked.

"I don't know; Betty just did it by herself!"

The Zevolra hovered over Caster's Court, curling up its wings and plummeting below. It squashed the marble fountain, flattening Akara's statue into dust and rubble. The debris flowed like a river from the heavy rain as the Zevolra lowered its head. Mozer grinned from behind the bone crown. "So you have a boyfriend? What's his—"

Wynn hurled a fireball the size of a carriage wheel at Mozer, but it dissolved into nothing upon impact of the crown.

"Keep trying, sweetie." Mozer chuckled. "This is hilarious. I take it the fate of Nezura rests in both of your hands? That's laughable. Neither of you are worth your salt compared to the Nobles. Not that they have much more worth, but they're a better challenge. Now come, girl, give me a kiss." Mozer pressed his face against the bone crown and puckered his lips with widened eyes.

All I could think of was Uncle Leopold dying at Mozer's hands.

"Do the spell!" Wynn commanded.

I couldn't get it started. *Mozer's eyes. That face.* Mozer haunted my psyche for many years, lurking in the shadows without me realizing it. It all resurfaced. *Uncle Leopold died because of his tyranny.*

"Max! The spell!" Wynn urged.

"I heard that." Mozer rolled his eyes. The Zevolra leaped forward like a playful cat to crush us, but Betty clutched Wynn and sprinted away. The park quaked as the Zevolra landed.

"I owe you my life!" I yelled at Betty.

The Zevolra spun around with surprising speed and jumped up, taking flight into the air again. "Watch your city get demolished!" Mozer howled as the Zevolra flew downtown.

"No!" Wynn shot up in the air and blasted past the front of the Zevolra, shooting multiple fireballs at the bone cage, but Mozer was untouched. The Zevolra swiped with its left claw and grazed Wynn's leg, causing her to spiral down.

Betty ran up to the edge of Caster's Court to get a closer look. I feared the worst—Wynn was about to collide with the Bone Tower—but a gust of wind rocketed from her heels. She recovered and bulleted back up towards the Zevolra. Throwing her hands forward, she charged an enormous fireball. The blistering, miniature sun exploded into a stream of flames, coating the entire bone prison. Mozer's shriek echoed through the city. The Zevolra groaned and flapped its wings backward.

"She did it!" Betty and I jumped in celebration, but my smile disappeared as Wynn fell to the ground. This time, she was lifeless. "Vlark! What can we do!" She plummeted, and just as she was about to disappear in the sea of buildings, she flipped herself upright and treaded in the air. The Zevolra steadied its smooth glide, but something caught its attention northbound. Wynn took it as a chance to fly away from the Zevolra and sped back to Caster's Court.

"Thank goodness you're alive! I was so scared!" I said, and Wynn collapsed in the two-inch layer of water covering Caster's Court.

"I'm exhausted." She grumbled.

"What happened over there? What got its attention?"

The Zevolra landed in front of the Nezura gate, standing in the wide-open field, holding its neck high. Mozer gazed below, smirking. Horses sprinted across the horizon. Lara and Holtmeyer led the two chariots in front with a battalion from the Silver Army racing behind.

"Well, Lara," Mozer boomed, "seeing as the king is still alive, they should follow my command if they don't wish to die! After all, they're still *my army!*"

The battalion pulled out arrows and spears.

Telyos stood at the top of Skull Tower, staring through the window slit in the circular chamber. There was no mistake; he saw his sister at the forefront of the army, and his heart sank. Tears escaped the corner of his eyes. It was her. *It really was her.* He wanted nothing more than to hug her. Maya stood beside him in the chamber, watching the commotion as well. He turned to her and bowed.

"Maya, I have to go. I hope you understand."

"Where to?"

"My sister has come, and I know Wynn told us not to do anything, but I'd rather die by her side fighting than sit here and watch."

Maya bowed. "Of course. I'll make announcements accordingly."

Wynn pushed herself up from the ground and darted her eyes north. "Max, I'm not sure what's happening over there, but the Zevolra is stationary. I've lost energy for any fire blasts, but I have an idea."

"What? Anything!"

"I need some time to recharge, but I can fly us over there in the meantime. While it's distracted, you have to pull off the bone-crushing curse on the crown. It's the only thing I can think of. Mozer is invincible in that thing. That should be enough time for me to regain my spark."

"Hold on! What do you mean, fly us over there?"

Without saying a word, Wynn took a deep breath and lifted Betty on her back while I was still on Betty's spine.

"What do you think you're doing?!"

Wynn soared into the sky with a gale-force coming from her heels. In an instant, the buildings in Nezura shrank, and I was hovering over the city with a bird's-eye view. The rain fell lighter the closer we were to the clouds. Wynn's flight arched like a rainbow, and we were getting close to the apex.

"Are you crazy?!" I screamed.

"Get ready to focus! We're about to descend! Then you have to crush that bone crown!"

"My beautiful Silver Army, you all know who your rightful commander is. Kill Lara and Holtmeyer! They're nothing but traitors! And then come claim Nezura with me! Relish in the glory of the day we've waited so long for," Mozer yelled from the top of the Zevolra crown. "I could've recruited you all for this battle, but I didn't, saving your lives! You all owe me!"

Lara held up a sword sky-high as the Silver Army aimed their bows, javelins, swords, and throwing axes directly at Mozer.

"I think you see where their loyalty lies," Lara yelled.

"Fine, go ahead, try it, attack me. Maybe then you can comprehend what you're up against!" Mozer shouted.

Lara boomed, "3. 2. 1. Attack!"

The Silver Army unleashed their weapons, cutting through the rain, but everything bounced off the resilient bone crown.

"Okay, that's enough of that. Now you're going to learn why you made a mistake. I'll make an example out of half of you." The Zevolra lifted its massive claw and hammered it down over the infantry.

"Bone lance!" a voice cried out. A brilliant green spike of light shot across the field, flanking the Zevolra from the side. It struck the Zevolra's arm before it could flatten the Silver Army. The monster groaned and recoiled until its back was against the gate.

"Are you kidding me? You can't handle a stupid spell!" Mozer screamed.

Lara saw who shot the bone lance, and her heart dropped. It was her brother, Telyos. He stood by himself as his knees wobbled and he collapsed to the ground.

"Stay here!" Lara said to Holtmeyer as she sprinted to her brother's side.

"Let's give this another try!" Mozer commanded, but the Zevolra quivered.

� ✦ ✦

"I'm going to have to crush the bone prison?" I yelped, arms still wrapped tightly around Betty's neck with every inch of strength. The view was breathtaking, but I couldn't admire the lime-yellow glow of Nezura on a rainy evening. I had to focus. I clutched onto Princess Nezalon's crown for a moment.

We reached the top of the arc, and I swore I saw a glimpse of the sunset through a tunnel of clouds. Maybe I was crazy, but at that moment, something magical happened. It was like I couldn't control my hands. I ripped out my uncle's ivory blade from my pocket and clutched it.

The words burst through my mind like a raging river through a dam.

Death comes to those innocent and guilty
I concoct the spell of greatest responsibility
It should never be the first, always the last
Resort. Contort. Crush. And demolish.
Or a structure no more can prosper
The only method I should foster
It can break barriers or walls
But its intent is always for all
Unity.
Toting the thin line
Of death and life
I take in, I ensure,
Virtue in my conjure
I wet my brush in death's goblet

The tip of the blade shined bright red, and I stabbed my hand, descending towards the Zevolra. The bone prison locked in my sight. Time stood still.

But this paint will create beauty in life.
This paint will create beauty in life.

A giant black cube zoomed around in my head, but it stopped just as it was about to knock me off balance. I saw Akara, Mr. Cole, and Uncle Leopold pushing the cube, causing the entire block to crumble. I stared at them in awe.

My head felt like it was submerged in muck.

"Uuuuuuuuuuu diddddddittttttttttttttttt!"

Our descent felt like a slow pull underwater.

"Youuuuuuu diiiiiid ittttttttttttt!" It was Wynn's voice but deeper than I remembered.

"Huh?" I blurted, but my voice rumbled my skull, nausea and vertigo created a lovechild that turned my brain into a sloshing soup.

"Youuuuuuu diiiiiid it!" Wynn cried out, the world rushing back to normal. Physics, gravity, time, and speed all came back to what I remembered.

"What!" I yelled, and it came out perfectly fine, but I'd never felt so tired in my life. My body felt like it had been wrung out like a washcloth.

"Look!" Wynn yelled.

The crown's spears cracked at the tip, the Zevolra let out a piercing shriek. The cracks expanded, jagged black lines invaded the crown, and spread throughout the rest of the body. It kept groaning, and Mozer screamed. The crown shattered like panes of glass, and the rest of the bones crumbled. The arms, the legs, the wings, the torso, the neck, and finally, the head all burst into shards.

Wynn gently landed Betty and me to the ground. Wynn collapsed upon setting foot on the earth, falling next to Telyos and a woman I recognized as the king's assistant, Lara. I slid off Betty, landing on my back. Every muscle ached with dull pain.

Mozer stood on a pile of broken bones and stared at his army without a glimpse of fear. His lips curled crookedly from ear-to-ear as the infantry prepared their bows, spears, and throwing axes.

"3…" Mozer counted down.

Holtmeyer arched his brow and threw up his sword. "Attack!" Holtmeyer hollered. The infantry launched their projectiles. Not every single toss was accurate, but the ones that hit Mozer bounced right off, and he chortled.

Mozer wandered over to Wynn and me, still on the ground. I wanted to scurry away, but I didn't have the energy. Betty grabbed Wynn and tried to pull her out, but Wynn batted away her hand.

"I have to stay! Pull Max away!" Wynn yelled.

Betty ran up to me and dragged me, but I said, "No, I must stay with Wynn!"

"Oh shut up, all of you. I'll kill you off one by one. Don't even worry about it." Mozer towered over Wynn and beamed.

"Fight me!" Lara charged after Mozer and threw a flurry of punches and chops, but Mozer dodged each one, smiling. It was effortless for him.

"You've had your fun." Mozer gripped Lara's wrist and threw her to the ground with pulverizing force. "I want to kiss the Vyrux. Can you imagine the power in those lips? I'm salivating at the thought. I must have them."

"Vlark you!" Wynn screeched, and Mozer's grin stretched tightly over his face.

The rain slowed until there was no more. I was sopping wet and motionless on my back.

Mozer stomped over to Wynn, and Betty charged with her skull lowered, but Wynn hollered, "No, Betty! Don't get in this fight. I can do this!"

"Aw, come on, eye for an eye, summon for a summon, it's only fair!" Mozer grinned at Betty.

Betty halted and backed away.

"Nevertheless." Mozer crouched down and clutched Wynn's throat, pulling her up until her feet hovered above the ground.

Wynn struggled for breath and squirmed in his grasp, but he didn't let go. Mozer beamed like a child receiving a birthday present. He pulled her down close to his face, his lips puckering and twitching.

Betty, Lara, Telyos, Holtmeyer, the Silver Army, and I all dropped our jaws.

With her free hand, Wynn formed a tiny fireball and threw it in Mozer's eyes.

"Ack!" He stammered backward, holding his hands over his face. "I wanted to make this fun! Fun for you and me!"

Wynn held out both of her hands in a triangle and blasted out a jet of roaring flames. Mozer was engulfed and shouted in anguish.

"This isn't how it was supposed to end! Nezura, Lavarund, the world! I hold the key!" Mozer croaked through the raging flames. He was still grinning, and his eyes were popping out of his head.

Wynn held her hands forward. The blaze streamed as tears fell down her cheeks. Her face was contorted with pain. She let out a scream before the fire died out, and she collapsed to the ground. Mozer's body was ablaze as he fell to his knees, glaring and grinning at Wynn. His skin became nothing but a seared crisp.

Everyone stood still.

Mozer fell to the ground as smoke plumed from his lifeless body. We all stared and waited for what felt like an eternity before anyone said a word.

"It's done," Telyos said. But with the way his voice pitched up, it sounded like a question.

Yes, it was done. This nightmare was over. That dreadful man would no longer be the ruler of Lavarund. His days of spreading hate and division were finished.

Mozer was charred, unrecognizable. The smoke disappeared from the body, but something made me squint.

The body twitched.

I thought I had hallucinated, but no. It twitched again with more force.

"He's still alive!" I screeched, and everyone gasped.

The body stood back up with jerky motions and movement. It stared directly at me. A piece of burnt skin chipped off from the mouth, revealing a grin.

Goosebumps scattered across my body, freezing my movement. Betty stood beside me and didn't react.

"Wynn, get up! He's not done!" I hollered, but she was still knocked out. "Wynn! No! We need you!"

The burnt body jerked in different directions as if possessed. It let out a guttural howl as more burnt pieces flaked off, revealing new, glowing skin.

The body had a curve that appeared more feminine than Mozer. Nor was there as much muscle mass as before. He appeared shorter. A black cloak suddenly covered the body, flowing in a breeze.

I gasped. "It must be the evil energy thingie! From the original Zevo—"

"Or maybe it's me." The face was revealed, one that I recognized. Younger than I'd ever seen. My jaw fell, and I couldn't help but cry.

This must be a dream. This is all a dream.

"Akara?!" Telyos beamed. "How did you—"

"Telyos." Akara bowed her head and walked towards us. "It's good to see you all."

Betty hopped with glee, sprinted to Akara, and squeezed her with a hug from her boney arms.

"Yes, yes, it's exciting to see you, too, Betty, believe me." Akara rubbed her back. The two of them walked over to me, and Akara crouched down. "I'm so proud of you, Maximilian. You did a wonderful job. You have a bright career ahead of you."

"Explain, now, please," I said.

Akara smiled. "I suppose everyone here deserves an explanation. Let me wake up Wynn first." Akara reached in my pocket and pulled out my uncle's dagger. "Sorry, I'm going to need this." Akara stepped over to Wynn and said an incantation. A blue light hovered over Wynn. Then one hovered over me, and my body's aches and pains melted away. I could move my arms and legs again.

Wynn picked her head back up. "Did we win?" she uttered and locked gazes with Akara, who was standing over her and reaching her hand out. "Oh no, don't tell me I died?"

"You didn't; you're very much alive, and so am I," Akara said. Tears spilled down Wynn's face as she grew the widest smile I've ever seen. Wynn bounced up and gave Akara the tightest hug possible.

"You're crushing me!" Akara forced out.

"Sorry!" Wynn put her down, sniffling and wiping the tears away with the back of her hand. "I just thought you were gone! And now you're here! It's a miracle!" She laughed, but her smile faded. "But what happened to Mozer?"

"He died. Allow me to explain what happened." Akara cleared her throat as we all listened closely.

"I performed the hardest necromancy spell I've ever done in my entire life. Necrocarnation. Believed to be a myth, and to be honest, I wasn't sure if I would be successful after seeing all the different futures. None of them guaranteed this triumph. Necrocarnation requires a brutally long incantation, immense focus, and another subject. You must have the understanding that your old body will die. Here's how it works. Your spirit is absorbed into your knife, and you stab it inside the subject. If done correctly, the knife disappears inside your target. But the tricky part is they must die within twenty-four hours for your soul to claim the body. And, bravo, you beat the tyrant Mozer within the limit, and I claimed his body at its current age. Good thing he was younger, right?" She giggled, a wonderful giggle which I longed to hear.

"So, what happens now?" I asked.

"A lot. The kingdom of Lavarund is yours and Wynn's now. Don't forget Lara, too, and her allies, they deserve something special. But you'll figure it out. As for me, I want to go back to my island to live out my days in peace and solitude." She held Wynn's hand and my hand. "Since I never had children of my own, please promise me you'll visit."

"Of course! We'll figure out a schedule!" Wynn beamed.

"Yeah, that sounds great." I nodded.

We pulled her in for a triangular hug.

"What should we do? How can we ensure a prosperous kingdom?" Wynn asked.

Akara laughed. "Don't ask me. You'll all figure something out. Enjoy your fame. If ruling a country really makes you uncomfortable, you can give it over to Lara and Holtmeyer. They seem honorable and benevolent. But as for me, I'm going back to my island."

"Don't you at least want to stay and say hello to the people of Nezura? They worship the ground you walk on; they'd be amazed to see you and what you've done," I said.

"Eh, that's okay. I'd rather live in the shadows undisturbed at my island. If something ever comes up, you two know where to reach me. I love you both. I'm proud of what you accomplished, and you should be, too. Have Telyos give you a Nezura town ceremony before you do anything else." Akara pulled Wynn and me in for one last hug. "See you both soon."

Akara walked to the west, and we watched her walk off into the sunset over the hills. The clouds had cleared away. Wynn, Betty, and I shared a heartfelt stare and put our arms around each other.

"We did it! We're heroes!" Wynn hollered. "Now we can each get a castle and do whatever we want!"

"What about Telyos, Holtmeyer, and Lara?" I asked.

"Castles for them too!" Wynn had tears streaming down her face again. "I'm just so happy."

Telyos and Lara walked up to us.

"Well done, you three." Lara smiled.

"I believe a ceremony is in order, yes?" Telyos asked.

"Sure," Wynn and I both said at the same time.

"I want some more mead. That stuff is delicious!" Wynn's lips curved up.

Telyos chuckled. "Let's go back to my house; there's plenty of mead for all of us."

After a long weekend of heavy mead consumption, hanging out with the Nobles, and enjoying my new place in Nezura, Wynn and I attended the ceremony on the Necromancer's Primacy that Monday at Caster's Court, which had been cleared of rubble and set up with a stage in the back.

Wynn, Betty, and I sat in black cushioned chairs in front of thousands of cheering people. We shared the stage with Lara and all the Noble Necromancers. Telyos stood at the podium.

"Thank you all for spending your holiday at this ceremony," Telyos announced. "Today, we pay tribute to the two people and dinosaur summon who saved Nezura. After spending time with these extraordinary individuals over the weekend, we reaffirm the belief that no matter who you are, even if you're a necromancer who isn't the best and struggles to fit in, you can achieve greatness. Or if you're going through a challenging period, be patient, and you will get through it; there are better days to come in the future.

"I would also like to apologize to Maximilian, someone who was never given the amount of time and care needed to blossom. We should have never let him go, nor should we have ever let anyone feel left out. With all that said, I would like to thank Wynn and Maximilian once again and give them two of the finest forged necromancer knives. Both of which are made with the bone remnants of the Zevolra. Please stand up and accept our gift."

I would never forget the sight; Nezura was alive with energetic people and summons, and the audience thundered with applause. Wynn, Betty, and I stood up, bowed, and accepted our rewards.

Standing next to Betty and Wynn, I felt like I was finally home and where I belonged.

When life settled down after the shock Lavarund endured with King Mozer, a lot had changed.

I had grown close to Wynn. The two of us continued staying at Akara's house that she gifted to us. Betty stayed with us too, and she even learned how to cook and clean, making life much easier for Wynn and me.

Lara and Holtmeyer returned to the castle, and we relinquished any ruling duties to them to handle. We felt it better for the citizens of Lavarund to have people they recognized as their leaders. As much as people were excited that Mozer was gone, supporters still worried about necromancers coming in and killing them in the middle of the night.

There was a lot of damage to be undone.

Lara was anointed queen, and Holtmeyer was her official assistant. The two of them immediately tried to dispel the rumors and hatred against the necromancers, but not much changed at first. Necromancers still lived in secret among society but openly lived in the Southeast. However, it was no longer against the law to practice necromancy. Books could be sold in stores, but only the towns close to the Southeast border accepted any texts. It would take some time for comfortability to spread.

Wynn grew fascinated with the idea of helping to implement change for a better Lavarund. Every day and night, she constructed ideas for an improved governing body over Mozer's regime. Lara and Holtmeyer promised that change would come and that they would happily collaborate with Wynn. This snowballed into greater responsibility, and Wynn moved out of the house to live in the Lavarund Royal Castle.

"Goodbye, sister," I said, my eyes brimming with tears.

"Goodbye, brother." She smiled as she silently cried. "And goodbye to you too, Betty." She hugged the pet summon.

Betty rubbed her back with her tiny arms.

"We should go visit Akara next week, maybe? If you're free?" Wynn asked.

I chuckled. "I haven't done a vlarking thing the past month and a half. Of course, I'll be there."

Wynn hopped on a skeletal carriage and headed towards the Royal Castle. Betty and I watched her go down the street before we returned inside to our humble abode.

What was I going to do with my life now? That was the constant question swimming through my mind. Even when Wynn asked me what I thought about doing after our life-changing event, I didn't have the slightest clue.

I thought about being a Noble Necromancer, but it seemed like a lot of work, and I'd have to sharpen my skills. At the time, I enjoyed relaxing at home, reading books, going for walks around the city, and watching some of the world's finest entertainment performed by skeletons. People often waved to me when I was out on the town, and it warmed my soul. Going into Risers, a handful of people always greeted and knew my name, for the right reasons.

"Hey! There's the city savior." Henry grinned from behind the bar. "The usual?"

I laughed. "Yeah, that'd be great."

I told Henry about Wynn moving away because she would accompany me sometimes when I went to Risers.

"Well, that's a damn shame. Wynn was a great person. So! What are you thinking about doing with your life now?"

I chuckled. "Why the vlark do you have to ask me that? I'm twenty-six, and I still don't know what I want to do with my life."

"It's not a race, Max, just remember that. One day, you'll probably be a yapping bag of bones just like me, except less annoying, of course. Or maybe more annoying." Henry winked. "But seriously, take some time for yourself. You're young."

"I already have, for the past month and a half. I'm starting to feel guilty."

"Don't worry about it. You received a gift of money from the city. You're basically royalty who's able to retire. You should be very grateful for that. Enjoy your life and do whatever you want because you went through a lot of vlarking madness. Take a vacation, maybe."

Henry was right. I owed myself some leisure travel. I had plans to go to Akara's island on Sunday, but I figured I'd do some exploring before then.

Betty and I trekked north of Nezura on Friday. We even made it all the way back to my old house in Verrenna. I received a few weird looks riding in on Betty, but I was fortunate that no one bothered me. When we pulled up in front of my house, I saw another family bringing in crates of food. My heart sank. I knew what it meant. When I checked by the cemetery, I found the graves of both of my parents.

It was strange. I thought I would cry, but I didn't. Even though they were biologically my parents, it never truly felt like it. Regardless, I paid my respects at the grave. *"Beneath the soil I call upon the underworld. Roots, stems, and leaves come out untwirled. Show me an ivory succulent or flower. With the Earth, I'm one with your power."*

Bone flowers sprouted up to my knees and danced gently in the wind next to their tombstones.

I smiled and put my arm around Betty. A thought crossed my mind. *Did Uncle Leopold have a grave in Lostonia?*

On Sunday, I visited the Lostonia cemetery, but I couldn't find Uncle Leopold's name. It was disheartening, but it made sense why they wouldn't give him the respect he deserved all those years ago.

Something had to be done.

Betty and I went to the docks of Lostonia after visiting the cemetery. Curmudgeon Carl took us out on the Bolt Sea until we arrived at Akara's hidden island home, protected by a magical layer of fog. When I made it to the house, I couldn't believe my eyes. Telyos, Lara, Holtmeyer, and Wynn were already drinking mead with Akara, who was beaming so brightly. I don't think I'd ever seen Akara that happy.

We enjoyed an evening of playing cards, drinking, and showcasing some summoning spells to watch as entertainment. Akara performed a dance number with a few other skeletons, juggling bones in rhythm as one of them played a marimba. We clapped when Akara finished and bowed.

"I thought you'd be learning the deep, unknown secrets the necromancers have yet to discover," I joked.

Akara grinned. "I don't know if you know this, but I have a lot of time on my hands."

Later, we had a bonfire at the center of her island; the stars and moon glowed bright up above. A gentle breeze tickled the flames, but no smoke blew in anyone's eyes.

I sat next to Akara, and Wynn sat on her other side. Akara turned to me and smiled while everyone else was caught up in a conversation about Orbavue or something. I wasn't paying too close attention.

"How have you been, Maximilian?" Akara asked.

"I think I'm doing pretty good. I don't know." I laughed, but my smile faded.

"Care to elaborate?"

"I felt so high after everything that happened. It was amazing to be recognized as an influential figure and hero of Nezura, but everything kind of died down. I mean, I feel a sense of accomplishment I don't think I've ever had, but—"

"But you're still craving more?" Akara lifted an eyebrow.

"I guess so. A steady stream of sustained worth would be nice, but I don't know how that would be possible. How many tyrant kings are running around for me to stop?" I cracked up.

"You don't have to go around stopping evil to feel a sense of fulfillment. Besides, the Zevolra core evil won't take shape for another thousand years."

"Well, I'll be long gone by then, but you might still be around." I snickered.

Akara smiled. "Maybe the Zevolra core won't take shape, now that the remains are destroyed. Time will tell."

A pause lingered between us before I said, "If you don't mind me asking, what's been some of the most rewarding moments of your life?"

Akara sighed. "Well, now that I'm in a young body again, I, too, have had a renewed drive in chasing accomplishments. But for me, venturing into the unknown territories of necromancy gives enough thrills. It's not for everyone—not that I'm saying you couldn't do it—but it can be challenging. Sorry, I'm digressing. To answer your original question, when I look back on my long life and career, some of my most rewarding moments came from teaching. Although you might not feel it right away, the difference you made becomes clear at another time in the future."

I nodded. I had never thought about that. "Good to know." I smiled.

"I'm delighted you're here tonight, Maximilian. I've never been a mother, but I imagine this is the type of love they feel for their children. I'm proud of you."

"Thank you." I hid my tears, but my sniffling couldn't be concealed.

The rest of the night wrapped up with people chatting over the bonfire. Apparently, a new figure came to prominence in Orbavue that had been getting a lot of controversial attention, but I didn't care enough to listen closely. Daydreams of how I'd spend my life kept me distracted. The idea of standing in front of a classroom and teaching a group of kids seemed invigorating. Especially coaching a student who struggled like me would be redeeming beyond anything else I could think of. That's all I ever needed, someone to believe in me, and I could give that back to others.

Another idea crossed my mind.

"Telyos, may I bend your ear for a moment?" I asked.

✖ ✖ ✖

Later that evening, when Akara returned to her house, and everyone else left, she retired to her bedroom and lay down. Parts of her body twisted and twitched involuntarily, like something trying to escape. Akara whimpered, for she knew what was coming.

A slithery whisper echoed in her mind, *"I'll find a way, Akara. I'll overthrow you from this throne and kill you a third time. They say third time's the charm, right?"* Mozer cackled. Akara sat up, sweating profusely as a stabbing pain stung her forehead. She screamed so loud it shook the windows.

Akara collapsed on her pillow, unconscious. When she woke up in the morning, her head ached. Still, she carried on with her typical day of studies and concentrated meditations.

✖ ✖ ✖

After my conversation with Telyos at the bonfire, a month passed.

I researched what was needed to become a teacher in Nezura. All I had to do was take a rigorous certification class. I enrolled that summer, anxiously awaiting the day where I could carve my path just as Akara did in education.

Telyos and the Noble Necromancers passed the motion to erect a new fountain on Caster's Court. Akara would stand proud once again but, this time, with a wall of plaques behind her. They would tribute those who were instrumental in stopping King Mozer. One of them honored Uncle Leopold, per my request.

When it was finished, I visited the memorial  and cried as soon as I saw the plaque.

Leopold Smith worked in Lostonia as one of the greatest blacksmiths of this generation. He lived as a regular citizen but designed knives and armor for necromancers when most blacksmiths in Lavarund wouldn't. Because of his open mind, Leopold learned the spells of necromancy to continue producing his work. He lived his life of necromancy in secret but exposed Maximilian Forrester, his only nephew, to the craft. When the public discovered Leopold was a necromancer, he was murdered by the tyrant Mozer. Leopold was never given a proper burial. For his bravery and kindness, we honor him.

The plaque was written with glowing ivory print on a smooth black marble wall. In front of it was a patch of grass.

"Beneath the soil I call upon the underworld. Roots, stems, and leaves come out untwirled. Show me an ivory succulent or flower. With the Earth, I'm one with your power."

Ivory tulips sprouted from the ground, sitting below the monument.

"If it wasn't for him, we'd never have met." I smiled as I patted Betty on the back. My eyes blurred with tears. "Sorry you have to see me like this. I'm an emotional sap. What can I say?"

Betty pulled me in for a hug.

"Thanks." I cleared my throat and sniffled. "We should go back home. I still have a lot of studying to do for my certification." I turned around and stepped over to the edge of Caster's Court and admired the horizon of Nezura. The bone tower, the Municipality Building, all of the other tall structures. The sun was setting, painting the ivory horizon a shade of gold.

Afterword

I originally posted this story on Reddit, and it was about 20,000 words. I'm excited it has grown into an entire novel with a sequel finished! Be sure to check out Tales of Nezura Book 2: The Sapphire Skeleton if you liked this novel. I think it's an even better adventure!

It's tough writing a book and publishing it. The hardest part is finally saying, "I'm done." Along with pushing past the self-doubt. I couldn't be happier that it's finished, and I'm grateful that you've read my story. Thank you. I wish I had something more interesting to say. Well, if you want to hear more thoughts of mine, reach out to me at randallfcooper12@gmail.com. Also, I'd love to hear your thoughts on the story. If you want to see a picture of my dog, I'll happily email you one too.

About The Author

I work in the educational sector in Southeast Michigan. When I'm not writing, I'm watching a movie or making one. And if I'm not doing any of those things, I'm probably making music.

Please join my website's mailing list at www.randallfloydcooper.com, and I'll let you know whenever there's a new release.

Acknowledgements

If it wasn't for my fans on Reddit and Patreon, I don't know if I'd have the confidence to publish something. I'd like to thank these people all over the world that have been so kind to me. They feel like a close friend. I can't believe the kind-hearted community I've cultivated on the internet (of all places)! Much love and appreciation for them.

Also, my family and close friends, thank you. Here are more people who I'd like to thank: Trevor, Ryan, Spencer, Riley, Jackson, David, Nick, Harry, Nan, Howard, Martin, Thomas, Steven, Elizabeth, Nick, Tyler, and anyone else I might be forgetting who has taken the time to support me.

Made in the USA
Middletown, DE
11 May 2023

30408661R00086